# FIND MY WAY
# BACK TO YOU

## MEL G

ISBN: 1542726484

ISBN-13: 978-1542726481

# Chapter 1: Dana

As I stood glancing around my new office, I couldn't suppress the smile that crossed my face. After much convincing and encouragement from my mother and best friend, I finally decided to take their advice and open up my very own event planning service. For the past three years, I had been working as the Executive Assistant to one of the top Event Planners and Promoters in Dallas. My ex-boss, Maxine, was great at what she did, but honestly, I had been the reason her company stayed afloat over the last few years.

Maxine had been going through a nasty divorce at the time and it really took a toll on her work. There was no way I was going to sit back and watch all her hard work go down the drain. Through blood, sweat, and tears, I had managed to triple Maxine's clientele and my hard work sent her reputation through the roof.

My best friend thought I was crazy for putting in all that work, only for Maxine to take the credit. I agreed, which is why I'm standing here in this office today. It was definitely a risky move and sometimes I regretted my decision to quit my job and go into business for myself. It also didn't help that I had zero clients at the moment. That's okay, though. Not many people knew about my company yet, other than my family and close friends. I had decided to throw a grand-opening party to introduce "Elite Event Planning." It was scheduled to take place two weeks from now and I was stressing out.

No matter how many event and parties I had put together, I was still nervous. This one was different. Instead of Maxine's, my name would be on this. Everything had to be perfect. One little screw up could possibly make or break me.

"Ms. Barnett," one of the movers called from the doorway. "Everything is done and put together. Is there anything else we can do for you?"

"No, that should be it. Thank you," I smiled politely and handed him a tip.

I followed behind him to the front to take a look at the furniture placement. I had given them simple instructions on the vision I had for the front area and they had done a great job executing. Walking over to the smoke-grey sofa, I plopped down onto the plush furniture and sank into the cushions.

"Girl, get your butt up. No time to be sitting on your booty," my best friend Morgan said jokingly. "How does it feel to be your own boss?"

"Terrifying," I laughed.

"I don't know why. This is what you do, Dee."

"I know, but this is different. I don't have Maxine's name to back me. No one knows who I am. What if I don't get any clients? I no longer have that nice check coming in every two weeks," I ranted. "Then, I just got my townhouse. What if I can't keep up with the mortgage? I can't depend on my savings. What if-."

"Dana, cut it out and I mean it," Morgan cut me off. "No one knows who you are? That's BS and you know it. Maxine might have gotten the credit, but best believe everyone knew who was putting in the work. Once word gets out that you've branched off on your own, they'll be beating down your door, throwing work your way."

"You think so?"

"I know so," Morgan replied confidently. "Now, get with the program, girly."

See, this is why I loved my girl. Besides my parents, Morgan was my biggest cheerleader. Whenever I began to doubt myself, she was always there to get my head back in the game. Morgan had been my other half since meeting at summer camp twelve years ago. We had formed a bond all those years ago, and been by each other's side ever since. Morgan was more of a sister to me than a best friend. I was even the godmother to her beautiful twin girls, Ryanne and Reign.

"Sooo," Morgan said dramatically. "Have you heard the news?"

"What news?"

"Your boo is coming back to town," she smirked.

"My boo? What boo?"

"Mr. Kenyan Spencer. That boo," Morgan said with a sneaky smile plastered on her face. "Word is, he's moving back. So, you know what that means, right?"

"Nothing at all, Morgan."

"Oh, come on, Dana. The chemistry between you two was undeniable. If he hadn't moved away, you two love-birds would still be together."

"Morg, let it go. What Kenyan and I shared was just a summer fling. Nothing more," I assured her. "Besides, that was almost six years ago. I'm sure he's moved past that and so have I."

"Listen, Dana. I'm your best friend and I know you. Your mouth is saying one thing, but your eyes are telling a completely different story. We both know you never got over him. I know what happened back then was hard for you to deal with, but you have to let all that go," Morgan placed her arm around my shoulder. "I just want to see you happy again, Dee."

"Morgan, I am happy," I weakly smiled.

Truth is, I wasn't and hadn't been for the last six years. At the time, I had just completed my junior year in college and was excited to be on break. Morgan had been offered an internship in Atlanta for the summer, so we weren't going to be able to hang like we usually did. Instead, I had to find something else to do with my time. That something just so happened to be Kenyan Spencer.

I had been leaving from the airport after seeing Morgan off and ran smack dab into him. Literally. My attention had been glued to my phone and I hadn't been paying attention to where I was going.

\*\*\*\*

*"Whoa. Careful there,"* a deep voice spoke as they steadied me.

*My eyes slowly trailed up until they landed on the lips that had spoken in that sexy baritone. Thoughts of all the things I could do with those juicy lips clouded my thoughts and temporarily paralyzed me. It wasn't until he cleared his throat that I snapped out of it.*

*"Are you okay," he asked again.*

*I looked up and got a look at his handsome face. My eyes widened in surprised.*

*"Dana?"*

*"Wow. It's been a minute. How have you been Kenyan," I inquired.*

*"I've been great. Man, it really has been a minute. Haven't seen you since graduation. You're looking good, girl," he nodded approvingly.*

*"So are you. I see you've been eating good," I acknowledged jokingly.*

*Kenyan had always been big in stature, but now he seemed huge. He stood at about 6'6 and I'm pretty sure be weighed about a solid two-fifty, if not more. Years of playing football had surely done his body some good.*

*"Hey, I have someone waiting for me," he said, breaking me from my trance.*

*"Oh, yea. Sure. Go ahead. I didn't mean to hold you up."*

He paused. "Would it be okay if I got your number? I would love to get together and maybe catch up."

"Yea, that would be nice."

Who knew that would have been the start of something great. Kenyan and I spent the entire summer together. He was staying at his older brother's place while he was back in town and instead of staying at my parents', a majority of my nights were spent there with Kenyan. We would spend all day out exploring the city and trying new things together. Then would spend all night exploring each other's bodies.

The thought of him leaving once the summer ended was the furthest thing from my mind, so when that time came, I was heartbroken. I knew that what we were doing had to come to an end eventually, and I was okay with that at first. However, what I didn't expect was to fall in love with him. My feelings for Kenyan snuck up on me and I didn't realize how deep they ran until I had to watch him board that plane.

After we both returned to school, our communication became almost non-existent. Our schedules seemed to never coincide. He was always busy with football and I was trying to juggle school and a part-time job. Things really changed after he was drafted. I drowned myself in work and tried to push him out of my head, but that was almost impossible.

*My mother made it her business to update me on everything Kenyan Spencer. If only she knew the pain that those memories of Kenyan and I brought on, she would surely stop mentioning him and trying to rekindle things with us. Morgan was the only person who knew about what had happened. Though she wasn't as pushy as my mother, she was still holding onto the idea that Kenyan and I would one day find our way back to each other.*

**\*\*\*\***

"Dee, I have to get going," Morgan said, drawing my attention. "Richard's about to lose his mind. The girls talked him into taking them to Build-A-Bear and the ice-cream shop."

I laughed because I could only imagine what Morgan's husband, Richard, had been through today. I loved my god-babies to death, but they're a very energetic pair and could easily wear a person out.

"Oh, lord. Yea, you need to go relieve my brother-in-law before the Tiny Twins have him over there in tears," I joked.

"Whatever. You better leave my babies alone. Are we still on for lunch tomorrow?"

"Of course. Your treat, right? It ain't cheap opening your own business, you know," I said, batting my eyes at her.

"Oh no, honey. Don't be trying to hit me with the puppy eyes," Morgan said, playfully pushing me away from me. "You know I got you."

"Thank you, bestie."

"Yea, yea. Whatever, chick. I'll see you later," Morgan said, kissing my cheek.

She was halfway to the door before she stopped and turned back to me.

"Promise me you'll think about what I said. I just want to see you happy."

I didn't have to ask what she was talking about because I already knew. Instead of having the same conversation over and over again, I simply nodded my head. Morgan could be a very convincing person when she wanted to be, but this wasn't something I was going to move on. Kenyan Spencer was my past and I planned on keeping it that way.

# Chapter 2: Kenyan

Stepping off the private plane, I removed my shades and looked around. It had been a minute since I'd been back in Dallas for something other than a game or a quick visit with my family. This time around I was home to stay. After suffering from my seventh concussion of my NFL career, I decided to leave the game and retire. A lot of people felt as though twenty-seven was too young to even think about retirement, but their opinions weren't what was important to me. My health was.

I had been experiencing some pretty intense migraines over the last year, which had begun to take a toll on me and effect my performance. After meeting with a few specialists, I made the decision to step away. It had already been on my mind and I would rather the choice be mine, rather than being forced by some sort of traumatic injury.

Don't get me wrong. I love football, but honestly, that's not all I wanted to be known for. I had a good run, but it was time for something new. I was still somewhat young. (I'm not sure if twenty-seven was considered old nowadays.) I was sitting on a decent amount of money, thanks to my mother. She made it her job to make sure I was smart with my money and invested wisely.

Other than purchasing myself and my parents a home, splurging on a car or two, spoiling the hell out of my parents, and making sure my siblings were straight, I barely touched my money. There were too many guys I knew who blew through all their earnings and barely could maintain their lifestyles by the time they retired. I didn't want that to be me.

"Superstar!"

I looked around and laughed when my eyes landed on my big brother, Kendrick. He removed himself from his position on the front of his truck and began to approach me with a huge smile on his face.

"You're looking good, lil' bro," Kendrick said, pulling me into a brotherly hug. "Let's hurry up and get out of here, because your mama has been blowing my phone up all morning."

I chuckled. "Oh, she's my mama now?"

"Hell yea. You know she don't be worried about anybody else when your ugly ass is home," he joked while helping me with the few pieces of luggage I had with me.

The rest of my things were scheduled to be delivered later this week, and that worked out perfectly. Being the procrastinator that I am, I had yet to find me a place here. You would think that I would already have something out here since it was my home state, but nope. Like I said before, I barely even came back to Dallas and my stay was always brief. It was either a hotel or my parents' house. Hell, they had more than enough room.

"So, what have I missed," I asked after we were settled in his truck and headed towards my parents' house.

"Not much. Kelsey is driving me crazy. You know she has a little boyfriend now," he said, referring to our little sister.

"A boyfriend? Since when?"

"I don't know, but his ass is always around. He be following Kelsey's ass around like a little love-sick puppy. They met at school," he informed me.

"Nah, I don't care where they met. If I ain't met him yet, then he ain't her damn boyfriend."

"Who you supposed to be? And besides, ma loves his ass and dad even cool with him. You don't run nothing, Ken," my brother laughed.

"Yea, whatever. How are my sis-in-law and niece doing?"

He ran his hand down his face and released a breath. "Both spoiled as hell. I swear I hope we're having a boy this time. I can't deal with another female in the house."

"Oh man, whatever. You love it. When do y'all find out the sex?"

"Next appointment," he beamed. "But I'm telling you, Ken. If that man tells me we're having another girl, I'm passing out in that room."

The serious look on his face had me in tears, laughing. I believe he probably would pass out in that damn doctor's office. For his sake, I really hope they're expecting a boy.

"So, I heard from my boy Rich that your girl just opened up her own event planning service," Kendrick spoke and cut his eyes at me.

"Who's my girl?"

"Don't play, Kenyan. Dana Barnett," he said. "You want to pretend like you don't know who that is?"

"I didn't say I didn't know who it was, but you said my girl like I'm supposed to automatically know who you're talking about."

"Well, you know damn well I wouldn't be talking about any of those ditzy broads you be bed-hopping with."

"Ditzy? Now you know I only mess with the best," I bragged.

"They straight, but they ain't Dana," he said turning to look at me completely. "Maybe you should look her up and take her out to dinner or something. Rich says she's single."

"How the hell does Rich know so much about Dana?"

"Calm down, killer," Kendrick laughed after seeing how tense I had become. "He's married to her best friend. I know you remember Morgan."

"Oh, yea," I said, relaxing. "I didn't know he was married. How'd she manage to lock him down?"

"I have no clue, but he's head-over-heels in love with that damn girl. You think Charli has me whipped, Rich is a thousand times worse. And they have twin girls."

"Oh, wow. Where the hell have I been, man?"

"I know right. We need to link up with the old crew and go out for drinks or something."

"Bet. Set that up," I nodded.

"I will, but don't think I didn't notice how you tried to change the conversation on me when we were talking about Dana," he said bringing the truck to a stop in my parents' driveway. "But I'll let it slide for now."

We both got out and before I could close the passenger door good, I was being bulldozed by my sister Kelsey and niece Karli.

"Uncle Ken!"

I almost had the cover my ears because of the loud screeching sound that Karli was making. I bent down and swooped her tiny frame up into my arms. She released a fit of giggles as I placed kisses all over her round face. I finally stopped and she was still laughing. Balancing her in one of my arms, I used the other to pull my sister into my side.

"I missed you, ugly," she said, wrapping her arms tightly around my waist.

"I missed you, too, bighead," I said, kissing the top of her hair.

"Dang, Kels. I don't get this type of treatment," Kendrick said walking up beside us.

"Because I see your mug every day. I don't have time to miss you," she said sticking her tongue out at him.

"Okay. Remember that."

"Nooo. I'm just kidding," she laughed. "You know I love you, too, big bro. I just missed my Kenny."

"Will you two get off him and at least let him make it inside the house first," my dad laughed from the front door. "He can barely even walk."

Once I made it to the porch, I let Karli down and greeted my dad.

"You're looking good son," he said hugging me.

"Thanks, old man."

"Old? Nall, young buck. I'm seasoned," he said opening the door for us all to enter.

"Kenny!"

I looked towards the top of the stairs to see my mom rushing down them, before she made it to me and threw herself in my arms.

"Oh, my baby's finally home," she smiled with tears in her eyes.

"Come on, ma. Don't start with the crying," I said pulling her tight into me. "You act like I never come home."

"Barely. Those quick little pop-up visits were different. My baby's home to stay."

"Ma, you're so dramatic," Kelsey laughed.

"This whole family is dramatic," Kendrick added. "Where's the food? I'm starving."

"What else is new," my mother laughed. "Breakfast is in the kitchen."

****

"You should really consider coming over for dinner, Kenyan. It'll be fun," Charli tried to convince me.

"What's fun about being the outcast with a group full of married people? I don't know if you got the memo, but I'm single as a dollar bill, Charli."

"Well, maybe it's about time you changed that. You're not getting any younger, you know?"

"You trying to call me old, Charls?"

"Of course not, but you will be by the time you decide to settle down," she said.

"Baby, you're wasting your time with that one," Kendrick said turning his beer up.

"No, I'm not. Kenyan just needs to find the right woman," she argued and turned her attention back to me. "Maybe I can hook you up with someone."

"Hell no. Thanks, but no thanks, Charli."

"Why not? You act like I have ugly friends or something," she scoffed.

"Didn't say that, but all of your friends are ready to walk down the aisle and pop out babies. I'm not."

"Unless it's with Dana," Kendrick mumbled but Charli heard him.

"Dana? Dana who? I know you're not talking about Dana Barnett," she smiled goofily.

"Yep, that's the Dana," Kendrick instigated.

"Whoa. What am I missing? Were you and Dana a thing?"

"Yep," Kendrick answered.

"No, we weren't," I said sending him a nasty look. "We just had a brief fling. That's it. I don't know why your messy husband trying to make it seem like something it wasn't."

"Because that's BS, Kenyan, and you know it. You two were madly in love with each other. Trust me, I would know. So stop with that 'it was just a fling' crap. You know it was more than that," he said.

"Bro, we were young. We've both moved on from that and I wish everyone else would, too. Dana ain't thinking about me."

As hard as I tried to convince my brother that I was over whatever it was that Dana and I shared all those years ago, I knew that was a lie. It didn't matter how many women I'd slept with over the years, I always found myself comparing them to her. We may have been young, but no one had ever made me feel the way she had.

Dana was everything and sometimes I found myself wondering how things between us would have turned out. We both were in two different states and had no idea how to make a long-distance relationship work. But like I said, I'm sure Dana wasn't worried about me and that little fling we had damn near six years ago.

"Are you listening to me, Kenyan," Charli asked with her hands on her hips.

"Yes, Charls. I'm listening."

"No, you weren't," Kendrick laughed.

"Man, shut up and stop trying to get me in trouble with your wife."

"Both of you hush," she chuckled. "I said that maybe we should find out whether or not Dana has been thinking about you tonight."

"Huh? Tonight?"

"Yep, tonight," she smirked. "The dinner's at Morgan and Richard's place and she's going to be there."

# Chapter 3: Dana

"Why do I have to come," I whined into the phone to Morgan as I searched through my closet for something to wear to dinner.

"Because you're my best friend and I said so," she laughed. "You're not doing anything else, Dee."

"And how do you know that? I could have a date tonight."

"Yea, right. When's the last time you've even been on a date? And don't even mention that disaster with Gerald, because that shouldn't be classified as a date."

"You're right," I laughed. "That was a disaster. Do you know he asked me to fly to his hometown with him to meet his parents?"

"No, the hell he didn't. Y'all only went out on, what, maybe two dates?"

"Exactly, but he had it in his head that fate brought us together and we were soulmates."

"Something was definitely wrong with that guy. I sure hope you deleted and blocked his number."

"No, I just told him that I didn't think things between us would work out. He still calls, but I always come up with some excuse to rush him off the phone. Hopefully, he'll get the picture soon and stop calling."

"Let's hope so," she said. "Have you found anything to wear yet?"

"Ugh. I'm looking now, Morg. I can't find anything."

"Don't play with me, Dee. You have a closet full of clothes over there that you never wear. I know you can find something."

"Or I could just stay home."

"Please don't make me come over there and drag you out. I'm not playing, Dana. You have a little over an hour, so get moving, missy," Morgan said before we ended our call.

Tossing my phone onto my bed, I turned back to my closet and huffed. I really needed to get rid of some of these clothes. I barely wore any of them anyway. After sifting through hanger after hanger, I finally settled on something to wear. We were just having a casual dinner at Morgan's house, so I didn't really need to be too dressy, but I couldn't just throw on a sweat suit either. Even if I wanted so badly to.

Morgan lived for these little dinner parties and I knew she wasn't going to be dressed down, so that meant I couldn't be either. She'd better be lucky I love her. I had recently purchased a pair of pink strappy Steve Madden pumps that I had been dying to wear, and decided to pull them out tonight. I paired them with a fitted blush-colored blouse, which I tucked into my navy high-waist trousers. My bob was freshly done and styled to perfection, thanks to my trip to the salon earlier. I placed my rose-gold MK watch on my wrist, before grabbing my nude clutch and heading to my garage.

Morgan lived in a gated community a few blocks from my townhouse, so it took me no time getting there. There were three cars parked in her driveway and it looked like I was probably the last to arrive. Shutting my car off, I grabbed the bottle of Merlot that I had stopped to get and headed to the front door. A few seconds after ringing the doorbell, Richard answered and took the bottle from me.

"Hey, Dana," he said pulling me into a hug.

"Hey, Rich. Y'all got it smelling good in here."

"You know how my wife gets down," he boasted, closing the door behind me. "Everyone's in the kitchen."

"Dana," Morgan said, stopping what she was doing and coming over to hug me. "About time you got here. I thought I was going to have to popup at your house for real."

"Morg, stop being extra. I'm not really even late. You said six and it's only 6:15. I'd say that was pretty good time."

"Yea, yea," she said waving me off. "You remember Debra and her husband Raul? And those are my co-workers Ginger and Sean. Oh, and of course Charlie, and I'm sure you know her husband, Kendrick."

I smiled politely and greeted everyone, before accepting the glass of wine that Richard offered me. Seeing everyone coupled up had me remembering the exact reason why I was hesitant about coming to this dinner in the first place. I didn't like feeling like a third wheel. Well, seventh in this case. LOL. I guess I would just have to make the best of it.

"How've you been, Dana," Kendrick asked. "It's been a while since I've seen you. You look to be doing well for yourself."

"She sure is," Morgan eagerly answered before I could. "She just opened her business. My girl is about to be the top Event Planner in Dallas, Texas."

I shook my head and laughed. I told you all my girl was one of my biggest cheerleaders.

"I've been great, Kendrick. I think Morgan just pretty much covered what I had going on right now," I joked.

"Congrats, girl. That's huge. I'm proud of you," he said.

"Thank you. It looks like congrats are in order for you two as well," I said motioning towards Charli's growing belly.

"Thanks, girl," Charli beamed while rubbing her stomach proudly. "I can't wait until we find out what we're having."

"If God has gotten any of my messages, it'll be a boy," Kendrick laughed.

"Hell, I'm praying with you. Trust me. I know your pain," Richard said patting him on the shoulder.

"Oh, y'all think y'all know pain. I'm the one having to put up with five spoiled ass women," Raul laughed.

"Oh, yea. Raul's ass has all girls," Richard shook his head. "Can you imagine having four daughters? I thought I had it bad with two. But four? There aren't enough guns."

"I know that's real," Kendrick said, high-fiving him.

"The food's done if you guys want to go ahead into the dining room," Morgan announced.

Much to my surprise, dinner was going great. I thought I would be the only single person in attendance, but as it turns out, Ginger and Sean weren't together. At least they weren't a couple, let them tell it.

"So, where's your boo, Dana," Ginger asked. "With as gorgeous as you are, I'm sure you have a few floating around somewhere."

"Nope, with as gorgeous as I am, I'm still very much single," I laughed.

"You need to let me change that," Sean flirted.

"Boy, she don't want your behind," Ginger laughed.

"See, why you always blocking," he said, playfully mushing her. "You just want to have me all to yourself. Don't worry, baby. There's enough Sean to go around."

These two were something else, but they surely kept me entertained. I was trying to control my laughter, when the doorbell sounded throughout the house.

"Baby, are we expecting someone else," Morgan questioned Richard.

"Umm, yea. Let me go get that," Richard said and discreetly cut his eyes in Kendrick's direction.

I don't know if anyone else noticed their exchange, but I surely did. I also caught the sneaky smile that Charli was trying so hard to hide. Something was up. It didn't take long for me to find out what that something was. Richard returned to the dining room with the last person I expected to see. My head whipped in Morgan's direction and she looked just as surprised as I was.

"Oh, man! You're Kenyan Spencer," Sean acknowledged excitedly.

"Stop acting like a groupie," Ginger whispered to him, before slapping his leg under the table.

"Sorry I'm late," Kenyan apologized and turned to greet everyone.

When his eyes landed on me, he stopped and held my gaze. His eyes were so intense that it was nerve-wrecking. Kendrick cleared his throat, pulling Kenyan from our stare down.

"You can sit over here," Morgan said, moving down one seat, so that there was an empty one between she and I.

I shot her a look and she returned a smirk. I felt extremely set up right now. Had I known Kenyan would be in attendance, this would have been the last place I would have come. Just by being in his presence for this short amount of time, he had me rattled. I didn't think he could look any better, but he proved me wrong. This man was gorgeous. Forget handsome. His features seemed to be placed so perfectly on his face and sculpted to perfection.

I discreetly admired him as he made his way over to the vacant chair. As big as he was, he still moved with the grace of a gazelle. Most people his size seemed somewhat awkward, but not Kenyan. He owned his size. His arm lightly brushed against mine as he got adjusted in his seat.

"How are you, Dana," his voice flowed out smoothly.

Lord, that voice. Kenyan's voice had always done something to me, and after all these years, it still had the same effect. A chill ran down my spine at the same time the vibrations of his voice moved through my body, hitting my most sensitive spots. I had yet to speak to him and it seemed like everyone at the table had their eyes on me, awaiting my response.

"I'm great," I finally released.

"Here you are, Kenyan," Morgan said, passing a plate his way.

"Thank you. I'm starving and this looks great," he said before bowing to say his grace.

"So, Kenyan," Morgan spoke after conversation had started back up. "I hear that you're back to stay."

"Yep. It was time for me to come back home. I've been away long enough. Besides, I was tired of my family sending threats every other week," he laughed.

"Oh, whatever," Charli laughed. "You know you missed us."

"He be frontin' like he don't, baby," Kendrick added.

"So, you all are related," Ginger questioned.

"These two knuckleheads are brothers," Charli informed her. "Can't you tell?"

Ginger glanced between the two of them before she slapped her forehead. "Well, how could I miss that. I didn't pay much attention, but you two are damn near twins. Wow."

"Are you really retiring," Sean asked Kenyan. "There's been rumors circulating, but nothing confirmed."

"Well, you'll have to wait until it is confirmed. You not getting no inside scoop around here," Morgan shut him down. "And he's not here to talk football."

"You always shooting a brother down, Morgan," Sean said throwing his napkin across the table at her. "It's not every day that I get to be in the company of one of the greatest athletes today. Let me have my moment."

Kenyan released a deep chuckled and I swear I thought I would melt. He sat his fork down and picked up his wine glass to take a sip. I watched from the corner of my eye as he swallowed the liquid and even the subtle movement of his throat was sexy. Why did it seem like everything this man did was perfect? I needed to get away from him.

"You okay," he leaned over and whispered, while resting his large hand on my leg.

I almost jumped out of my skin from the contact, but I managed to keep my cool. I nodded and quickly excused myself from the table so that I could go to the powder room. As soon as I was behind the privacy of the door, I drew my back against it and released a breath that I haven't realized I was holding. I needed to get myself together. All I had to do was make it through the rest of dinner and I would be okay.

"Come on, Dana. Get it together," I coached myself.

There was a knock at the door that interrupted my pep talk. Oh my god. I hope like hell it's not him on the other side of this door.

"Dana, are you okay," Morgan asked in a hushed tone.

"I'm good, Morg."

"Well, open the door."

I unlocked the door and opened it so that she could enter. She crossed her arms across her chest and stared at me. I tried to ignore her at first, but I knew she was waiting for me to ask her why she was looking at me like that.

"What, Morgan," I sighed.

"Don't 'what Morgan' me. Why did you run away from the table like that?"

"I didn't run away from the table, Morgan. I had to use the bathroom."

"Girl, tell that mess to someone who doesn't know you. You were running from that man and you know it."

"Did you know he was going to be here?"

"Nope, but even if I did, I still wouldn't have told you. You would've come up with some excuse as to why you couldn't make it," she said. "Stop acting like a wuss, Dee."

"A wuss? I am not acting like a wuss. It's just weird being around him after all this time."

"Only because you're making it weird. He seems perfectly fine being around you. In fact, his eyes have been all over you since he stepped foot through that door."

"He's not worried about me, Morgan," I said, more so trying to convince myself.

"I wish you would quit saying that. You better get with the program and hop back on that fine, chocolate, Greek-God in there. Hell, if I wasn't happily married to my sexy husband, I would be all over his ass. But since I am, I need you to get on it."

I washed my hands and shut off the lights, before pushing pass her. "You need help, Morg," I laughed.

"And you need to get laid, Dee. I'm just trying to help a sister out."

By the time we both took our seats, everyone had already finished with dinner and Richard was cutting into the chocolate cake that Debra and Raul brought.

"You want a slice, Dee," Richard asked.

"I do, but lord knows I don't need it. I'm already trying to drop a few pounds," I told him.

"Girl, where," Debra asked. "I wish I was your size."

"I know that's real. Dee, you're like the ideal size," Morgan co-signed.

"Well, my tight jeans are telling another story. Shedding a few pounds wouldn't hurt," I told them.

"I think you look great," Kenyan spoke while eyeing me. "Perfect, as a matter of fact."

I blushed and shied away from his gaze. "Thank you," I spoke lowly.

"It's about time for us to get out of here. We left the girls with Deb's sister and I know they've about worn her out," Raul said, helping his wife from her seat.

"Okay. Thank you, guys, for coming," Morgan said, standing to hug them both. "Oh, and thanks for that cake. It's delicious."

I had Richard wrap me up a piece of cake to take with me as I gathered my things.

"It's about time for me to head out too. I have an early day tomorrow," I told Morgan. "It was good seeing everyone."

"It was good seeing you, too. We should meet up for lunch one day this week," Charli suggested.

"That sounds great."

"Well, I'll see you all later," I said, rising from my seat. "I'll call you when I make it home and get settled, Morg."

"Okay, babe. Be safe."

"Let me walk you out," Kenyan said, standing along with me.

# Chapter 4: Kenyan

Dana was just as beautiful as I remembered her to be. I loved the style that she was wearing her hair in now. Back then, she had long hair that flowed down her back, almost reaching the top of her backside. Now, she sporting a short bob that framed her round face perfectly. It gave her a more mature look, if you asked me.

I managed to somewhat keep my cool during dinner and not make a fool of myself. I knew she was going to be here tonight, so I had already prepared myself for our encounter.

From the look on her face when I first entered the dining room, I could see that she was shocked to see me. We hadn't been in each other's presence since that morning I boarded the plane back to Florida. We had Facetimed a few times after I got back to school, but that didn't last long.

I placed my hand on the small of her back as I walked her out front to her car. Though she tried her best to hide it, it was nice to see that I still had that effect on her body after all this time. The slightest touch from me had her breathing uneven and I could feel the subtle chill that ran down her spine.

"Well, this is me right here," she spoke, motioning towards her black Nissan Maxima. "Thank you for walking me out."

Dana was looking everywhere but at me and I could sense that she was nervous being out here alone with me. She tried to open her car door so that she could get inside, but I gently placed my hand on her arm to stop her.

"Why are you in such a rush to get away from me," I inquired jokingly.

"That's not it. I just really need to get going. I have to get up pretty early in the morning."

"Five minutes talking to me isn't going to throw you off that much, is it," I questioned with a raised brow. "We didn't get a chance to really talk at dinner. How've you been?"

"I've been fine, Kenyan. Just busy working."

"I've heard through the grapevines that you've just started your own business. That's huge, baby girl. Congrats on that. Maybe I can treat you to a drink or something to celebrate," I suggested.

"Thank you, but that's really not necessary. It's not that big of a deal," she replied modestly.

"The hell it isn't. I can remember us sitting up all night talking about you opening your own business one day, so I know how much it means to you. Come on, Dana," I said, taking her hand in mine. "How about this. We can exchange numbers and whatever day works for you, we can link up."

"Fine," she finally agreed.

I couldn't contain the smile on my face as I waited for her to finish putting her number in my phone. She called her number from my phone, before handing me mines back. Since I got what I needed, I felt comfortable with letting her leave, without feeling like I wouldn't see her again. I pulled her door open so that she could get in.

"Since you have my number now, call or text me to let me know you made it home safe," I instructed her.

"I will. I'm not too far from here, so it won't take me long to get there," she told me.

"Okay, I'll still be waiting," I said, closing her door and stepping back so she could pull off.

"So, did you get her number," Morgan spoke from behind me.

"Dammit, Morgan," I laughed while grabbing my chest. "You scared the hell out of me. I didn't even hear you come out here."

She threw her head back and laughed. "Sorry about that. Did you, though?"

"I got this, Morgan," I chuckled and walked back towards the house so I could say goodbye to everyone.

I had accomplished what I'd come here to do and now the only thing left to do was go home, well my parents' house, and wait for Dana to call me.

\*\*\*\*

"You mean to tell me you don't like this one," I asked with my arms folded across my chest.

"I mean it's okay for a bachelor's pad, but don't you think you need a little more room?"

"Kels, I am a bachelor," I laughed at my sister.

My realtor had called me early this morning with a few listings that she wanted me to see and Kelsey begged me to bring her with me. If I had of known she wasn't going to be any help, I would have left her where she was. Out of the four places we've seen this morning, Kelsey didn't like any of them.

"You don't plan on being a bachelor forever, do you," she asked. "I'm just saying, bro. I think you need to find something that gives you room to grow. Who knows. Maybe sometime in the near future you'll find a nice woman to settle down with and maybe have a couple kids."

I stopped walking through the condo and looked down at my sister. "You sound like your mother. Did she put you up to this?"

Kelsey looped her arm through mine and rested her head on my shoulder, before resuming our tour. "No, she didn't put me up to it, but I can't say I don't agree with her. With the rate you're going, even I'll be married with kids before you."

"No, the hell you won't, Kelsey," I said pulling my arm away from her. "You're twenty. The only thing that should be on your radar right now is graduating. Not marriage and damn sure not kids."

"Be quiet, Kenny. You know what I mean," she said hitting my arm. "Are you anti-marriage or something? Kendrick says that there's only one person that you'd consider marrying. Is he talking about Dana?"

"Why the hell does this family have to always discuss my business? Don't you all have something better to do," I asked, laughing. "And how do you even remember Dana? You only met her like twice."

She shrugged. "Mama and Kendrick were talking about you two one day. They think that you guys are meant to be together and that's the reason why you haven't settled down with anyone, because you're waiting for her."

I shook my head as we joined my realtor in the living room. This conversation would have to wait. I was curious to know what all my mother and brother had to say regarding me and my relationship status.

"So," my realtor asked with eager eyes. "How'd you guys like this one?"

"This won't do," Kelsey answered before I could. "He needs something a bit bigger. How about we veto the condos and lofts, and check out a few houses."

"Umm," my realtor, Hagen, said looking for my approval.

I nodded letting her know that it was okay.

"No problem. I have a few that I can show you," she informed. "If we don't find what you're looking for today, I can put together something for later this week, as well."

"Sounds like a plan, Hagen," Kelsey said as she heading for the door so we could leave.

I guess Kelsey called herself taking over the appointment. I didn't mind though. I trusted her taste and had no doubt in my mind that she would help me find the right place.

\*\*\*\*

Just like I thought, Kelsey had helped me find the perfect home. Now I can admit that I wasn't sold on purchasing a big house at first, but I had finally got on board. Hagen ended up taking us to see a beautiful five-bedroom, four and a half bath house that was close to the neighbourhood that my parents lived.

The home had a three-car garage, a huge swimming pool and jacuzzi, a basketball court, and a decent-sized yard. The kitchen was immaculate and I could already picture my mother coming over to take over and have dinner parties here. It was equipped with state of the art appliances and plenty of room to make a mess.

The lower level of the home had its own gym, theatre room, and an additional room that I could already envision to be my mancave. Maybe Kelsey was on to something with that whole space thing. Yea, the house was big, but not overwhelmingly.

I had just finished all the necessary paperwork and received the keys from Hagen, making me a new home-owner. I owned a few pieces of property here and there, but this was different.

This wasn't just some condo that I'd purchased for when I was in town or something. I didn't even purchase a house when I was living in Miami. This was a whole house. A house that I planned on making a home. I could already see myself hosting the holidays here. Before, I never really pictured myself to be the type, but now I looked forward to hosting gatherings and having my family and friends over.

"Hello, mother," I answered my phone.

"Well, there's my son."

"Ma, you're acting like I haven't been staying at you guys' house for the last two weeks," I laughed.

"Yea, but you've been ripping and running so much that I've barely even seen you."

"I know, ma. I've been trying to get a few things in order and then on top of that, I just closed on a house this morning."

"Oh my god, Kenny! Already? Where's the house? I want to see it," my mother said eagerly.

"Calm down, woman," I chuckled. "You'll have your time to see it. I want to get someone over to furnish it first. I was thinking about asking Charli. You know that's her thing."

"That would be a great idea. You know that child has an eye for design. I told your brother he should talk to her about maybe considering to do it professionally. She could make some really good money."

"Sounds like it could be a good move," I agreed.

"Have you eaten lunch yet? I was about to go in here and whip up something for your father."

"No thanks, ma. I was actually going to call a friend and see if she wanted to join me for lunch," I informed her.

"She, huh?"

Dang. Why did I have to say that? I should have known she was going to pick up on it. Now, she was going to want to ask a million and one questions.

"Yes, she, ma."

"Well, who's this woman? Do I know her?"

"Ma," I sighed.

"What? I'm just curious," she said innocently.

"Too curious," I told her. "But I'll talk to you later. Love you."

Scrolling through my contacts, I smiled once I came across the name I was looking for. I pressed dial and waited for our call to connect. I hope she wasn't too busy today.

"Hello," her sweet voice answered.

"Afternoon, baby girl," I greeted. "I hope I'm not interrupted anything."

"Good afternoon to you too, Kenyan," she returned. "And no, you're not interrupting. I was actually about to order me something to eat while I had a free moment."

"I can think of something better. How about you let me treat you to lunch," I suggested. "That's actually what I was calling you for anyway."

"I guess that's fine. Where should I meet you?"

"I could just come and get you. Where are you?"

"You don't have to go through all that trouble. I don't mind driving," she told me.

"Dana, if it was trouble, then I wouldn't have offered. Now send me the address to where you are so that we can go eat. I skipped breakfast this morning, so I'm starving."

She agreed to text me the address to her office and I told her that I would be there within the next twenty minutes. I don't know why, but I felt like a teenaged boy getting ready to go on his first date. I don't even think this would qualify as a date. We were just two old friends about to grab something to eat. Granted, two old friends that used to share wild, passionate sex.

See, no. If I was going to make it through lunch, I needed to clear my mind of all sexual thoughts regarding Dana. However, that was easier said than done.

# Chapter 5: Dana

After exchanging numbers at Morgan's that night, Kenyan and I had been in constant contact. Whether it be through text or brief ten-minute phone calls. I always woke up to 'Good Morning' or the 'thinking of you' texts. We hadn't gotten the opportunity to go out for drinks yet, because we both had been extremely busy this week.

This lunch was about to be our first time seeing each other since the dinner. I wasn't as nervous today as I was that night. I was more at ease since we had been talking, so things didn't feel weird.

"It's about time he asked you out. I thought I was going to have to call Mr. Spencer to see what the hold up was," Morgan joked as I tried balancing the phone between my ear and shoulder.

"Girl, hush. You act like we're going on a date or something. We're just catching lunch, since we both were about to eat anyways."

"I get so tired of you, Dana. It's a damn date," Morgan argued.

"Whatever you say, Morg," I laughed.

The sensor on the front door sounded, announcing the arrival of someone. More than likely it was Kenyan, since I hadn't really put the word out about my business yet. I was still in the process on securing a few contracts and wanted everything to be in place before I started taking on clients.

"Talk to you later, Morgan. My lunch date is here."

"Tell Kenyan I said hi," she said before we ended our call.

Shutting down my computer, I grabbed my thin cardigan and slipped it on. It wasn't too cold outside, considering we were in Texas, but the winter months made it cool enough to want to cover my arms. I grabbed my purse and keys and headed to the front to meet Kenyan.

My breath caught in my throat at the mere sight of him. He was standing in the middle of my waiting area looking rather delectable. Kenyan could make just about anything he wore look good, but this navy pen-striped suit he was sporting today had me weak in the knees. In my opinion, there was nothing sexier than a man in a suit. Especially a well-tailored one that fit his body to perfection.

Kenyan finally turned in my direction after he finished admiring the random artwork that adorned the walls. Why was this man so damn gorgeous? I mean, this had to be illegal. It just had to be. I don't think any other man walking this earth looked as good as Kenyan looked right now. And that smile. Lord Jesus, that smile!

"Hey," Kenyan greeted as he approached me. "You're looking beautiful today."

Blushing, I tried my best not to waver under his gaze. "Thank you. You ready?"

"Yea. After you," he said opening the door and waiting for me to exit.

I locked the door behind me, before following him to the car parked directly in front of my office. For a moment, I stood staring at the car in awe. I had seen one at an auto show that I went to with my dad a few months ago, so I knew that it was the new Rolls Royce Wraith. I was never really into the flashy, expensive cars, but if I had the money, I wouldn't mind splurging on this here beauty.

"I take it you like the car," Kenyan joked.

"Like it? I love this freaking car! Oh, man," I exclaimed excitedly.

Kenyan chuckled and walked me over so that he could open the door for me. The all-white interior with black details matched the white-on-white exterior of the car. I was almost afraid to sit down. Luckily, I wasn't wearing jeans. I couldn't afford to damage anything in this car. It was probably worth more money than I'd seen in my lifetime. As a matter of fact, I was certain that it was.

"Why are you sitting over there like you're scared or something?"

"Because I'm not trying to mess up anything in this expensive car, that's why," I answered seriously.

"Relax, Dana," he tried soothing me. "I assure you that you won't destroy anything."

I finally relaxed and began to enjoy the feeling of the heated seats beneath me. Did I tell y'all this car was amazing? If not, then let me go ahead. This car is amazing! It felt like we were gliding through traffic. This was the one time that I was in this downtown Dallas traffic and wasn't about to lose my mind.

Kenyan and I ended up eating at Y.O. Ranch Steakhouse, which I'd never visited prior to today. He swore they had some of the best dishes and honestly, he was probably right. He talked me into trying to Chicken Fried Lobster and it was undoubtedly one of the best things to ever bless my tastebuds. The food was delicious. If I could, I would have tried everything on the menu.

Lunch with Kenyan was just like old times. It surprised me how comfortable I felt with him. Maybe Morgan was right. Things only seemed awkward at first because I was making it that way. We spent the entire time talking and catching each other up on everything that had been going on in our lives.

Even though I'm sure my life wasn't quite as adventurous as one of a famous athlete, he seemed to be genuinely interested in listening to me talk. By the time we made it back to my office, neither one of us wanted to part ways.

"I really enjoyed lunch with you, Dana," Kenyan spoke.

"I did as well."

"I have a few things that I need to handle, but would it be okay it we got together later this evening? Maybe we can grab a drink or two," he suggested.

"I would like that," I smiled.

"Great. I'll call you later to figure out what time works for you," he said after I had unlocked my office door and stepped inside. "I guess I'll see you later, Ms. Barnett."

"That you will, Mr. Spencer."

He placed a gentle kiss against my temple and retreated through the door we had both just entered. I stood watching him until he was back in his car and driving away.

For the remainder of the day, I tried focusing on work, but my mind kept finding its way to Kenyan. He was consuming my thoughts. Every little thing reminded me of him. It didn't help that his scent still lingered in my office. Even after all this time, he wore the same scent: Calvin Klein. I remember spending hours laid up under him, inhaling his scent. He always smelled so delicious. Almost edible. Well, I guess one could say that he was indeed edible, depending on how you looked at it.

Stop it, Dana! I didn't need to be having these thoughts. I already had to change my panties when I first returned from lunch. Kenyan had that effect on me.

Instead of sitting around pretending to be working, I decided to wrap things up early and head to check on my parents before I went home. I always tried to stop by at least once a week to spend time with them. Our relationship was extremely close and always had been.

Both of my parents were retired school teachers and spent a lot of their free time traveling and exploring the world. They took a vacation almost every other month. I hoped to one day be like them. They were carefree and enjoying life with the person they loved. That was like the perfect fairy-tale life, if you asked me.

Pulling up at the home that I'd grown up in, I pulled my key out and used it to let myself in. I could hear gospel music playing in the background, along with my mother's humming. I deposited my purse onto the table in the foyer and slipped out of my shoes.

This was always the routine whenever I came over. This was and would always be home for me, so it was nothing for me to make myself comfortable.

"Hi, Daddy," I said, walking over to the recliner he was rested in, reading the paper.

I placed a kiss on his cheek and sat on the arm of his chair.

"There's my favorite daughter," he smiled.

"I'm your only daughter, Daddy," I laughed.

"Still my favorite," he chuckled. "How've you been, sweetheart?"

"I've been great. Preparing for the big launch party coming up. I'm a little nervous about it."

"I don't know why. Dana, you worry yourself too much about things that you shouldn't. We both know that you're great at what you do, so don't second-guess yourself."

"I know, Daddy," I nodded. "But you know there's always that ounce of doubt that floats around in the back of our head."

"Well, it need to stop floating. I can't wait until you get everything up and running. I've been bragging to just about everyone I know and they can't wait for the grand-opening."

"Thank you. I can't wait either."

"Is that my baby girl I hear in here," my mother said as she rounded the corner, coming from the kitchen. "Hey, baby!"

"Hey, Mama," I said standing up so that I could hug her.

"Well, aren't you looking cute today," she said, checking out my clothes. "Who did you get all dolled up for?"

"Ma, I am not dolled up. I've been at work all day."

"That's not what I heard. A little birdie told me that you had a lunch date with a certain somebody that just so happens to be a very handsome, very single, football player that you once had a thing for."

"You and that little birdie really should find something else to talk about," I laughed.

I should have known Morgan was going to call and tell my mom about Kenyan taking me out for lunch the minute we got off the phone. That child couldn't hold water. If I knew those two like I thought I did, they were already planning the wedding. Don't get me wrong, I loved that my mother and best friend were so close. The only thing I didn't like was the fact that they were always going behind my back trying to conjure up some ridiculous plan.

"Oh whatever, child," she said, shooing me. "So, how was lunch?"

"I was nice. He took me to Y.O. Ranch Steakhouse. You and Dad should really go there one day. Their food is amazing."

"You hear that, Daniel? You have to take me to that fancy steakhouse, now," she told him, before turning back to me. "A friend of ours was telling us about that place and says they're pretty good."

"Yea, maybe after my first big contract, I can treat you guys."

I hung out with my parents for a little while longer, before I got up to head home. Kenyan had already texted me a little while ago and we agreed to meet up for drinks at eight. That gave me about three hours to get myself together.

The bar that Kenyan had chosen was an upscale one, so I wasn't quite sure what I needed to wear. I wanted to be comfortable, but I didn't want to be too underdressed. As much as I hated to admit, I needed Morgan's expertise. She had a knack for putting together the perfect outfit for any occasion.

"Are you sure about this one," I asked Morgan, as I stood in front of the mirror.

"Of course. You look absolutely stunning, best friend. If I was into chicks, I would definitely date you. Kenyan's not going to be able to keep his eyes off you. And if you're lucky, maybe his hands either," she winked, suggestively.

Slapping my hand over my face, I shook my head at her. "I can't with you, Morg."

"You say that all the time," she said, waving me off. "But seriously. That outfit is perfect. It's not too little and not too much. It says sexy, but not slutty. Flirty, but not desperate. You're good."

"Thanks for coming over at the last minute."

"Girl, you know it's nothing. Besides. I needed to get out the house for a minute. I think Rich's trying to get me pregnant again."

I burst out laughing. "What makes you think that?"

"The fact that he can't seem to keep his hands off me. Every other second he's trying to bend me over the furniture," she huffed. "Plus, I heard him on the phone talking about he can't wait until he has a junior."

"Well, what's wrong with that? I thought you wanted a big family."

"I do, but the twins are barely three. I love my babies, but they're a handful. Twins run in Rich's family and I would absolutely die if we wound up pregnant with twins again. I would rather wait until the girls are at least a little older."

"Maybe you should just talk to Richard about it. I'm sure he'll understand."

"I hope so. I have to lock the door just so I can shower in peace," she laughed. "I love making love to my husband, but that man is insatiable. They say your sex life dwindles once you have kids, but that's a damn lie."

"Oh, lord. I don't want to hear all that," I said, jokingly covering my ears.

"Honey, please. You act like this is something new. I'll be happy when you let Mr. Spencer get up in that again, so you'll have some stories to tell."

# Chapter 6: Kenyan

The sexy little chocolate bartender had been eyeing me since I sat down at the bar. She wanted me. The flirtatious looks that she was casting my way every few seconds were a dead giveaway. As tempting as it was, I was going to have to pass. She might have been easy on the eyes, but I'm sure she had nothing on my date for tonight.

"Can I get you anything, handsome," the bartender asked, finally making her way over to me.

She made sure to put emphasis on "anything." I smiled politely and gave her my order. When she turned to make my drink, I couldn't help but admire the way her bottom sat up in the fitted black slacks her wore.

A black clutch was placed on the bar next to where I sat, causing me to pull my eyes from the bartender's derriere. My eyes traced up the caramel colored arm that was perched on the bar, until they landed on the most beautiful creature to grace this planet.

Dana was absolutely breathtaking. The strapless black dress that she wore hugged her body in all the right places and stopped just below her knees. There was a split going up the middle that provided me with a glimpse of those gorgeous legs of hers. Boy, what I would give to have them wrapped around me again.

"Wow," I finally found my voice. "I know you're probably already tired of hearing me say this, but you look beautiful, Dana."

"Thank you, Kenyan."

There she was blushing again. Every time I gave her a compliment she would always shy away from me. There was this sort of innocence about Dana that I found incredibly sexy.

The bartender returned and handed me my drink, but I noticed that she didn't approach with the same bubbly attitude that she had before Dana arrived. I guess that must have ruined whatever plans she thought she had for me.

"Looks like I might be stepping on someone's toes," Dana said, tilting her head in the bartender's direction. "I think she had her eyes on you."

"Too bad, because I only have my eyes on one woman," I said grabbing her hand.

Dana visibly tensed up for a moment before she relaxed under my touch. For the brief two weeks that we had been back in contact, I kept things strictly platonic between us. I knew she was hesitant about reconnecting with me and I didn't want to scare her away. But for some reason, I was feeling brave tonight. I needed to get a few things off my chest and let her know how I felt.

"How about we find us a table to give us a little privacy," I suggested.

We both grabbed our drinks from the bar and began to scan the crowd for a table. After finding one, I placed my free hand at the small of her back and guided us through the crowd. Once we were settled, I felt comfortable enough to approach the subject at hand.

"Dana," I began.

She stopped bobbing her head to the soft R&B that played throughout the lounge and gave me her undivided attention. Even under the dim lighting I was able to admire the radiant glow of her skin. I got so consumed with taking in the sight of her that I almost lost focus on what it was I wanted to discuss.

"Yes, Kenyan," she asked with curious eyes.

Okay, Kenyan. Now is your chance. All I had to do was tell Dana how much I had missed her all these years and wanted us to give it another shot. It was simple. I just needed to shake these nerves off and man up. I mean, Dana had to be feeling some of what I was feeling at this moment. Our chemistry was undeniable. She just had to be feeling the same. Right?

Here I was. One of the most sought after bachelors and I was freaking out of the inside over sweet, innocent, little Dana Barnett. It's not like I was hard up for the attention or companionship. Women loved me. There was always a constant battle amongst women who felt they deserved a shot at being on the arm of the infamous Kenyan Spencer. Or even just in my bed. I never had any issues in that department. So, for the life of me, I couldn't understand why the idea of Dana rejecting me was so terrifying.

It probably had a lot to do with the fact that I never had the urge to pursue anything serious with any of those other women. None of them made me consider settling down and starting a family, or even being faithful. I've never been a player or dog; nothing of that nature. I just like a variety and never saw the point of being with one person. Except with Dana. She changed everything for me. Even during our brief fling, or whatever we were classifying that as, I never felt the need to give another woman my attention. Dana was all I needed, all I wanted, and that shocked the hell out of me.

Honestly, that had been the reason why I had pulled away from her once I returned to school. Instead of being man enough to tell her that I wasn't ready for a serious relationship, I chose to take the cowardly way out and blame everything on time and scheduling. I knew with the type of person that Dana was, she wasn't going to pressure or nag me about not giving her attention. So, what did I do? I chose to be an asshole and neglect her until our spark eventually fizzled and we went our separate ways. That's one of the only regrets I have.

Placing my glass on the table in front of us, I grabbed Dana's hands in mine and looked into her captivating chestnut eyes. The look on her face let me know that she was a bit nervous about what I was about to say. I couldn't blame her either.

I took a deep breath and went for it. "I know we've been getting reacquainted with each other and trying to build sort of a friendship, but honestly, I want so much more than that. I can't speak for you, but I still get that same feeling deep in my gut whenever I'm around you. I always find myself captivated anytime I look at you. Man, Dana, you've been all I've thought about since that night at Morgan's."

She pulled her hands from mines and her gaze shifted nervously. "Kenyan, you're only thinking about me like that because we haven't seen each other in a while."

"No, Dana. Even before I came back, you were all I thought about. It doesn't matter who I've been with through the years, I've always found myself comparing them to you, but no one could ever come close."

"Kenyan, we were young. It's not like we were actually in a relationship. We just dated for the summer and enjoyed each other's company," she replied, still avoiding my eyes.

"Really, Dana? We were younger, not young. Meaning old enough for me to know that you were what I wanted in a woman. I realized I wasn't ready for what you had to offer then, but I am now. We were great together, Dee. You can't even deny that."

"Yea, we were," she agreed. "But that was the past. I'm not the same girl I was six years ago and I'm sure you're not the same guy. We both-."

"Of course you're not. You've grown and matured into this beautifully amazing woman. That time to grow into our own is the best thing that happened, if you ask me. To be honest, I knew I probably wouldn't have been the best to you back then, so I'm sort of glad things happened the way they did. Now couldn't be a better time."

"For who, Kenyan? That may have been what was best for you, but it was pure torture for me. You can't even begin to understand what I went through. You just couldn't, Kenyan."

Staring at Dana, I knew there was more to that statement that she wasn't saying. Something much deeper. I knew that we had gotten pretty cozy during that time, but from the sound of it, I might not have realized the extent of our coziness.

"Dana," I said, lifting her face by her chin so that she was looking at me. "Talk to me, Dee. Make me understand."

"I was in love with you, Kenyan," she confessed. "And you left me. Left me to deal with everything alone. When I needed you the most, you weren't there."

Her revelation stunned me into silence. I didn't know what to say. It wasn't because I didn't have a clue to how she felt, but it was different hearing it. Dana never expressed those feelings to me. She kept them bottled up and tucked away. That was what made it easy for me to walk away. I felt like if she hadn't put it out there, it didn't exist. I didn't have to deal with it. I didn't have to face my feelings for her and try to define anything. It was easier not knowing.

The only thing was, I wasn't that same young-minded boy anymore. Now, I wanted to hear those words fall from Dana's lips. I needed to hear it. Why? Because I, too, had fallen in love with Dana. I think the moment I realized it was one night when we were laid out on Kendrick's living room floor, eating pizza and watching movies. She was telling me about all the big plans she had after graduating, and the raw passion I saw when she spoke of her dreams drew me in further. I knew then that she was someone I would be proud to have on my arm as my woman. As my wife.

The moment that thought crossed my mind, I nutted up. There I was, barely twenty-one years old and thinking about a damn wife. That scared the hell out of me. It was then that I decided to slowly pull away from whatever it was Dana and I were doing. I could already see myself madly in love with her, with a house full of kids, living the domestic life. Talking about scared my young ass almost to death. Those feelings were foreign to me. Of course I had been around love and healthy relationships my entire life, my parents being one of them, but the idea still terrified me. I had never felt so strongly about someone before.

"I know the way things ended was messed up, and I take full responsibility. Instead of talking to you and telling you how I felt, I sort of just ceased all communication and never looked back," I said, shaking my head. "That was wrong of me. Truthfully, Dana, I was scared."

"Scared of what?"

Now it was my turn to avoid eye contact. Rubbing my hand across the back of my neck, I focused my attention on the floor.

"Of loving you," I finally told her. "Those feelings weren't one-sided, Dee."

Her mouth fell open in shock, but she quickly recovered. "Lo.. Loved… You loved me?"

"Yes. Is that hard to believe?"

"Well, yea. It kind of is."

"I know my actions said something completely different," I nervously chuckled. "You were the one for me, though, Dana. You still are."

"Kenyan, were practically strangers. You don't want me. You want who I was six years ago and that girl is gone."

"And I'm VERY aware of that. I want the woman sitting in front of me. It's not like I'm asking for your hand in marriage. I just want the chance to show you what I KNOW we could be. I just want a chance. I'm not trying to rush you into anything. If you want to take things slow and date, get to know each other better, then we'll do that."

Disbelief. That's what I was feeling right now. I couldn't believe I was sitting here practically begging Dana for a chance. I didn't care though. I knew what I had to gain and I was prepared to go all out to get what I wanted. Who I wanted. I had nothing but time on my hands. Even if she chose to reject me now, I already had a game plan on standby and ready to be put into action. I wasn't stopping until Dana was mine. She was worth the effort.

"Okay, Kenyan."

That snapped me from my thoughts. "Wait. What? Okay? Okay what? Like okay, okay," I asked, trying to contain my excitement.

"Like okay, we can date and get to know each other," she chuckled, I'm sure at the excitement in my voice.

I guess I wouldn't have to pull out Plan B after all. Y'all just don't know how happy this woman just made me. All she said was that we could date, not be in a relationship, but date, and here I was ready to jump for joy like I had just won the lottery. In a sense, I had.

I had been given a second chance and I didn't plan on messing this up. Dana had better get ready because I was about to date the hell out of her.

# Chapter 7: Dana

Kenyan was really going all out with this whole dating thing. He made me make a list of things that I've always wanted to do and we were slowly checking things off. It wasn't even just that. We had a set movie night where he would come over and we would sit up all night watching endless movies and pigging out on junk, like we used to do. Every morning he would have flowers, along with breakfast sent to my office after he realized I had a bad habit of skipping meals. He made sure that I had no excuse as to why I wasn't eating.

A few days out of the week, when both of our busy schedules permitted it, he would stop by to take me out to lunch or bring lunch to me. We had been spending almost every free moment we had together. These last two months with Kenyan had been quite refreshing.

I didn't realize how nice it felt to have someone that made you genuinely happy. My work had consumed my life for so long that I never really bothered to date. To be honest, Kenyan was really the only person I had ever dated. I mean, I went on a few dates here and there, but no one ever really grabbed my attention enough to date them consistently. No one, but Kenyan. We just work. Things weren't forced between us and we didn't have to fake it.

"I'm sooo ready for tonight. I need this break," Morgan said as we walked through Macy's.

"You? Ever since launching, I've been having business coming from every direction. Don't get me wrong, I'm thankful for that, but it's crazy. I had to look into hiring an assistant and everything," I told her. "So, yes. This night is much needed."

"Well, I hope you're ready to party because Ginger is a wild one," Morgan laughed. "Girl, her birthday party last year was insane. I'm talking ass everywhere; every damn body was beyond drunk. I'm surprised I didn't get pregnant that night with the way I came home and attacked Rich."

"Oh, lord. I'm not so sure now," I said jokingly. "Maybe I need to sit this one out. You know I never did the crazy partying."

"Girl, please. You need to let your hair down. Who knows. Maybe you'll get so messed up that you'll give Kenyan some," she said, sitting to try on a pair of shoes. "I'm still curious as to why you haven't bust it open for him yet. It's not like y'all haven't done the do a million times before. Throw that punpun for a real one."

Looking around the store in embarrassment, I slapped Morgan on the arm. "Stop being so loud, putting my business all out in the streets," I laughed. "Don't you worry about what Kenyan and I do. Everybody can't be a hoochie like you."

"Honey, I'll be a hoochie, slut, thot, freak, and whatever else my husband wants me to be. He can get that," she said, sticking her tongue out at me.

"Hurry up so we can get out of here before you have these old people in here looking at us crazy, with your potty-mouth ass."

"Oh, but I'm the one with the potty-mouth," she said, side-eyeing me.

\*\*\*\*

"Do you know what club you all are going to," Kenyan asked as I stood in front of the mirror trying to finish my makeup.

"I forgot what Morgan said the name of it was," I spoke into the speaker of my phone.

"Oh okay. Well, let me know when you find out and be careful. You know it's a bunch of crazies out here."

"I will. What do you have planned for tonight?"

"Some old teammates are in town and I'm supposed to be going out for drinks with them. We may end up at a club. I'm not sure," he informed me.

"Okay. Have fun and you be safe, too. Don't go getting into any trouble."

"Trouble? Who me," he asked, feigning innocence. "Won't be no trouble this way. I'll be on my best behavior, baby."

"You better be."

"If it's not too late when you get in, can I come over?"

"Yea, that's fine," I told him. "But I'll talk to you later when I make it back home. I think Morg just got here."

"Okay. Talk to you later, love."

I smiled and ended the call. Butterflies still fluttered throughout my stomach every time Kenyan called me baby, sweets, or love. He was always so endearing and affectionate.

Shaking my head, I put my makeup down to answer the door, so that Morgan could stop laying on my doorbell. She was just so extra.

"If you don't stop ringing my doorbell like you've lost your mind," I snapped playfully as I swung my door open.

"Girl, whatever. I have to pee," she said, flying pass me.

Laughing, I closed the door and resumed what I was doing. I was putting the finishing touches on my makeup when Morgan appeared in the doorway.

"Damn, you looking sexy tonight, best friend," she complimented. "A little too sexy. Don't make me call and tell Kenyan on you."

"Whatever, you little snitch. My outfit is not that sexy and I'm sure Rich didn't get a good look at you before you left, while you're talking about me."

"For your information, he did. Which is why I was running a little late," she winked. "His behind followed me to the garage and bent me right over the hood of the car."

"You two are just nasty."

"Child please. Ain't no such thing as nasty when you're married," she waved me off. "You ready?"

"Ready," I said, grabbing my clutch and shutting off the lights.

Morgan wasn't exaggerating when she told me that Ginger was wild. I believe that was probably an understatement. Clubbing wasn't really my thing, but I thought I could at least hang. Ginger showed me just how wrong I was. I couldn't hang with her at all. She was up dancing to every song the DJ played and didn't look to be slowing down any time soon.

The only time she seemed to take a break was when she was searching for another drink, then it was back to dancing. I had to admit she was lots of fun, though. A little too much, but fun nonetheless.

After dancing for about two songs straight, I decided to take a break and find a seat in the section that Ginger had designated for her party. The shoes I had worn tonight were cute, but they weren't ideal to be dancing in. Not only did I need a break, but my feet did as well.

I was sitting on one of the sofas, nursing my drink, when I noticed commotion going on in the crowd. I wasn't sure what was going on, but I wasn't about to get up to find out. That's how people get hurt. I'm was just fine staying right where I was.

One of Ginger's friends, Kristen, came over and sat on the couch next to me.

"What's going on over there," I asked her.

"Girl, they say it's supposed to be some ball players over there. I don't even know. Them heifers almost bulldozed me over. I had to get from over there," Kristen said, pouring herself a cup of the 1800 tequila Ginger had gotten for us.

My heart rate accelerated as soon as she said that. There were plenty of ball players in Dallas, so she could have been talking about anyone. However, Kenyan did say he and a few of his boys were going out tonight. I mean, what would be the chances of us ending up in the same club?

Morgan and Ginger appeared through the crowd and were heading back to the table. I'm just going to go ahead and take back my previous statement. From the goofy look on Morgan's face, I'm guessing the chances of Kenyan and I winding up in the same club were very likely.

"So, guess who just strolled up in here," Morgan asked, plopping down on the other side of me.

"Who, Morg," I said, already knowing the answer.

"Your man. That's who."

"Wait. Who's your man, girl," Kristen asked, being nosey.

"Nobody."

"Kenyan Spencer," Morgan spoke at the same time I answered.

"Dana, if your ass don't quit playing and claim that damn man," Morgan fussed.

"He's not my man, Morgan. We're just dating. It's not like we've made things between us exclusive or anything."

"Oh, yea," she said, folding her arms across her chest. "So you mean to tell me that he could have a chick all over him, and that would be okay, since y'all aren't exclusive?"

"He has the right to do that. We're not in a relationship."

She pointed across the club to where the VIP sections were. "I'm guessing that's okay then."

I looked in the direction she indicated and my mouth dropped at the sight in front of me. Kenyan was seated in their section with a few guys who I didn't know, but from their build, I could tell they were football players, too. There were a few women in their section, and even more standing by security trying to gain access. I glanced at Kenyan and noticed the scantily clad woman who had made herself a little too comfortable on his lap. I waited for a few seconds to see if he would tell her to move, but when he didn't, I felt myself becoming upset.

"I'll be back. I need to use the restroom," I told them as I began to stand.

"Uh huh," Morgan said, shaking her head.

As I stood to my feet, I steadied myself before I made a move. The few drinks that I had were starting to get to me. I was preparing to head towards the restrooms, but for some reason, I had the feeling that someone was watching me. When I looked up, Kenyan and I made eye contact across the club. Instead of holding his gaze, I broke contact and continued to the restrooms. He had yet the get that chick off his lap. Granted he didn't look to be interested in anything she was saying, she was still there. I needed a moment to clear my head.

Surprisingly there wasn't a wait and the restrooms seemed to be fairly empty. After relieving my bladder, I washed my hands and stood staring in the mirror for a moment. It was time for another pep talk if I planned on making it through the rest of the night.

"We'll probably be leaving soon. Ging has had a little too much to drink and I want to make sure she gets home okay," Morgan informed me.

"I'm not that drunk, Morgan," Ginger hiccupped, while slurring her words.

I laughed. "Sweetie, you're definitely a little on the tipsy side. I-."

A pair of arms sliding around my waist from behind caused me to stop midsentence. There was no questioning who they belonged to. The scent and the smirks Morgan and Kristen sent my way were dead giveaways. I politely removed his arms and stepped out of his embrace so that I could turn to face him. From the looks of it, he'd had quite a few drinks himself. His hooded eyes were filled with lust as he took in the what I had on.

"Damn, sweets," he said shaking his head as he licked his lips. "You look stunning, baby."

"Thank you, Kenyan."

"What you doing coming out in this dress? This is too sexy. The sexy you only wear when you're on my arm," he said, running his hands up my thighs until they both found their way to my waist.

He pulled my body close to him and buried his nose into the warmth of my neck so that he could inhale my scent. I needed to get away from him before I forgot that I was mad at him for having some random woman sitting on his lap like she belonged there.

"Kenyan," I said, gaining enough strength to pull away from him again. "We're about to leave."

"Okay. Text me when you get in. I'll probably be right behind you. It's still okay if I come over tonight, right?"

"You think that's a good idea?"

"Huh? Of course I do. Why you ask that?"

I motioned towards the VIP section that he had come from, and at the woman who was still sitting there waiting for his return. He noticed what I was hinting at and shook his head.

"Dana, trust me. She's nothing for you to worry about. Just some groupie who attached herself to me the minute we stepped through the door," he explained.

"That groupie seemed mighty comfortable on your lap."

Kenyan stepped closer to me and pressed his lips to my ear. "You jealous, sweets," he asked, before beginning a trail of kisses down my neck. "If you know like I know, you would know that you have nothing to worry about."

"Bye, Kenyan."

He released me so I could leave with my group. Before I walked away, he grabbed my hand.

"Wait up for me, sweets. I'm right behind you."

# Chapter 8: Kenyan

"I'm about to get up out of here," I told my boys as I shook hands with all of them.

"Aight. I'll get up with you later, fam," my former teammate, Brodie, said.

"Aye, Kenyan," another one called out.

"What's up, Tate?"

"Who was lil' mama you were over there all hugged up with? That's you?"

"Hell yea that's me. That's wifey," I told them.

"Oh, it's like that? I see you, big dawg," Tate said, slapping hands with me. "Baby girl's a good luck. You should put in a good word for me with one of her friends."

I nodded in agreement and told him that I would. I was headed out of the section when the chick from earlier stopped me.

"Leaving so soon? Where you headed, baby?"

"Home," I replied, keeping it short.

"How about I join you? I can assure you I'll be great company."

"No thank you, baby girl. My lady's all the company I need. You enjoy the rest of your night," I said and walked away.

She must had been out her mind if she thought I was about to take her home with me. I haven't even given her any indication that I was interested. Yea, I let her sit on my lap, but that was only because I was feeling a little too good from the drinks I'd had and really wasn't paying her any mind. I'm sure seeing her on my lap was the reason that Dana kind of played me to the left tonight.

That's exactly why I was trying to get out of this club and make it to her house. I didn't want to allow her time to think on it. Then all sort of things would be floating around in her head. I needed to nip all that in the bud before it even got there. We were in a good place right now and I didn't want a bad decision while being intoxicated be the reason for us taking ten steps backwards.

When I pulled onto her block, Morgan was heading down the street and honked her horn as she passed. Good. That let me know that she hadn't been home long enough to really get settled. Unless she went straight to her room and dived face first into bed, she was awake. If I knew Dana like I thought I did, she was going to want to shower before turning in for the night. She had this thing about getting into bed after being out and not showering.

There weren't any lights on inside, from what I could see. I quickly cut off my car and jogged up to her front door. It seemed to take her a few minutes before she finally answered. I could see now why she took so long. From the towel wrapped snuggly around her and the water dripping from her body, I could tell that she had already been in the shower.

"What are you doing here, Kenyan," she asked as she tried to shield herself behind the door.

"What do you mean? I told you that I was coming. Did you think I was saying it just to be saying it?"

"No. I just figured that you had somebody else to occupy your time tonight," she said, avoiding my gaze.

"Don't do that, Dana," I told her. "Are you going to make me stand out here all night or let me in?"

She slowly opened the door wide enough so that I could step inside, before closing and locking it behind me. I didn't allow her time to think or react as I grabbed her around the waist and lifted her into the air.

"Kenyan, what are you doing," she squealed, as she instinctively wrapped her legs around my waist. "Where are you going? Put me down."

"I'm taking you back to the shower. That's what you were doing before you answered the door, right," I asked, as I walked through her bedroom and into the attached bathroom.

I slid her slowly down my body until she was back on her feet. After turning the shower back on, I removed my shoes and began to undress. Dana stood unmoving, her eyes following my every move. It wasn't until I removed my shirt that she finally snapped out of whatever trance she was in.

"What do you think you're doing, Kenyan?"

"What do I think I'm doing," I asked before dropping my pants. "I don't know, but I can tell you what I KNOW I'm doing. I'm about to take a shower with my woman."

"Your woman?"

"Yes, my woman," I said stepping into her personal space and pulling the towel from her body. "You got a problem with that?"

She shook her head no. I guess I had put her on mute after I removed my boxers. The way she was eyeing my package, you would have thought she'd never seen it before, let alone had it inside of her. Swooping her back up into my arms, I opened the shower door and stepped inside. Luckily, Dana had a spacious shower with a built-in bench inside.

Taking a seat, I made sure to position her so that she was straddling my lap. Her breathing had picked up and she was trying her best to keep her composure, which I'm sure was difficult with my erection coming to life under her.

"Kenyan," she whined as I placed my hands on her hips and began to slowly move her back and forth in my lap.

"Yea, baby," I asked, while leaning forward to bite her nipples.

"Oh, god," she moaned as her head fell back. "Kenyan, baby, wait."

"Wait for what, baby? Huh," I asked as I began to grind her harder into me.

From the wetness dripping onto my lap, I knew she was more than ready. I placed one of my hands to her center so that I could delve in her essence. One of her hands flew to grab my wrist the moment my fingers entered her. She was trying her best to get me to stop but I wasn't about to let up. Making a come-hither motion, I attacked her G-spot. She was close. I could feel it. The constant contracting of her walls and the look of pure ecstasy on her face were a dead giveaway.

"Cum for me, sweets. Let it out," I urged.

"No, baby. Please! Give me a second, Ken," she pleaded, trying to remove herself from my lap, but I had a firm grip around her waist.

"I'm not letting you go until you do what I said."

"Oh my god, Kenyan! Ughhh," she cried out as she released her creamy goodness onto my hand.

Removing my fingers, I quickly placed them into my mouth and sucked them clean. It had been too long since I had the pleasure of having her on my tastebuds.

"You want to know why I call you sweets," I asked as I watched her come down from the high of her orgasm."

"I think I have an idea," she answered breathlessly.

I quickly washed our bodies, before turning the shower off and wrapping us in towels. I gently laid Dana in the middle of her queen-sized bed, before going over to her dresser to grab her lotion. Starting at her feet, I began to massage every inch of her body. It might sound corny, but Dana really was perfect in every sense of the word. At least she was in my eyes. I could sit and look at her body all day and not tire. Everything about her being enticed me.

The constant moans escaping her mouth weren't helping matters either. My mans was rocked up something serious right now. As much as I wanted to cater to her body right now, I don't think I was going to be able to restrain myself much longer. My body was feigning for hers and itching to become one. I needed to be inside her. Now. Slowly kissing up her body while she laid on her stomach, I stopped once I reached her ear.

"You good, baby?"

"Mmhmm," she mumbled, with her eyes still closed. "Why'd you stop? That was feeling good."

"Because I'm struggling back here," I said, pressing my lower half into her backside.

She inhaled a sharp breath as a deep groan slipped from her lips. Involuntarily, she pressed her bottom back into me.

"Shit, sweets," I groaned into her hair. "I need you, baby."

She ground her hips back into me again, but this time with intent. I took that as the greenlight to continue. I placed my hand between her legs to make sure that she was ready for me. I wasn't surprised at all when I came across the flood that had formed there once again. That's one thing I loved about Dana. She was always ready for me.

Placing my head at her opening, I slowly began to enter her. Damn. I don't remember her feeling this good. I thought she had me before, but man. The way her body was gripping me, welcoming me, had my mind gone. It took everything in me not to bust early. I had never been a minuteman and I wasn't about to turn into one now. I took a moment to get myself together before pushing all the way inside of her. Once I hit rock bottom I stayed there. I didn't move. My entire body was completely still for at least a full minute. I needed a second to marvel in the softness.

Once I was confident that I had myself under control, I finally moved. Drawing back, I braced myself before thrusting back deep inside her. Dana gasped and gripped her sheets tight.

"Uhhh," she moaned, before burying her head into her covers as her body convulsed.

One stroke. That's all it took for Dana to release all around me. From that reaction alone, I could tell that her body hadn't been taken care of in a while. Probably not since the last time we'd been together. It didn't matter though. It was my mission to leave my mark. No other person would ever get the chance to please her body. She was made for me and only me. Our bodies were so in tuned with each other that it was almost frightening.

"Baby, wait," she cried out as I assaulted her spot. "Hold on!"

"Come on, baby. You should know better than that. Don't act like you forgot," I teased, while stroking her deeper. "I'm not stopping, so you might as well give me what I want."

"I can't cum again," she whined, while trying to run from me. "Slow down, babe."

That wasn't about to happen. Pulling out, I flipped her over onto her back and slid back between her legs. I threw her legs onto my shoulders before entering her again.

"Now tell me you can't cum again," I said as I hit her with a death stroke.

Her mouth fell into an "O" but nothing came out. Tears formed in the corners of her eyes as her nails dug into my forearms. Speechless. Not a sound. I was hitting it so good that she was crying.

I wasn't a cocky guy, but I knew what I was working with and I knew it was lethal. I hope Dana didn't have anything to do tomorrow because she was about to be out of commission after I finished with her. I felt her gushy walls clenching around me and knew that another orgasm was close.

"Give me one more and I'll be good. One more, sweets. Cum with me, baby," I coached, feeling my peak nearing.

I let her legs down from my shoulders, allowing her to wrap them around my waist. The urge to be as close to her as humanly possible consumed me. Dropping my body flush against hers, I pinned her against the bed as I delivered powerful blows to her uterus.

"OH, GODDDD!"

I covered her mouth with mine in an attempt to muffle her screams. The last thing I needed was to have one of her neighbors calling the police because they thought I was over here killing her. Oh, I was murdering something, alright, but not in the sense that they would be thinking

She bit down on my bottom lip and tightened her legs as she released one final time. The euphoric expression that graced her features is what sent me over the edge. With one more hard thrust of my hips, I released everything I had into her. My body collapsed and it took me a moment to remove myself from her. That right there just drained almost every ounce of energy I had left in me.

Finally, I mustered up enough strength to get up to use the bathroom and clean myself up. Grabbing one of the extra wash clothes, I wet it so that I could clean Dana as well. I couldn't help but shake my head at the sight in front of me when I returned to the room. Dana had already rolled over onto her side and was curled up in a ball, snoring. I guess I didn't need to ask how I did.

As gently as I could, I cleaned between her legs and returned the rag to the bathroom, before returning to climb back in bed with Dana. Snuggling up behind her, I pulled her into my chest and rested my arm around her waist. I could get used to sleeping like this every night. My eyes were getting heavy and slowly drifting closed when something crossed my mind. I wonder if Dana was on birth control, because we damn sure didn't use any protection.

# Chapter 9: Dana

I think I'm going to have to cancel lunch plans with my mom today. There was no way I was going to make it. I could barely make it down to my kitchen this morning. After waking up in the middle of the night TWICE for another round, Kenyan had my body screaming. I couldn't even take a step without feeling the effects of our lovemaking. A nice hot bath was definitely on my list of things to do today.

"You don't have to sit over there looking all pitiful," Kenyan laughed as he placed eggs on the plates in front of him.

He felt bad for the damage that he'd done to my body, so he decided to get up and fix us breakfast. It wasn't like I could do it anyway. My little lady was so sore and swollen that even the slightest movement had me wincing in discomfort.

"Shut up, Kenyan. You're the reason I'm sitting here looking pitiful," I complained.

After he finished plating our food, her brought our plates over to the island where I was sitting and sat them down.

"I'm sorry that I hit it so good that you can't walk this morning, baby," he said, placing a kiss against my forehead and sitting next to me.

"That was some apology," I said, sarcastically.

"Well, that's all you're getting. I shouldn't have to apologize for making you feel good. Would you suggest that I just stop, altogether?"

"No," I answered, pouting.

"Okay, then. Stop complaining and eat," he laughed. "What do you have planned for today?"

"Well, I was supposed to be meeting my mom for lunch, but I really doubt if I'll make."

"I really am sorry, baby. I should have taken it easy on you. I know it's been a minute since you had somebody put it on you like that."

"You make me sick," I said, throwing a piece of my toast at him.

Kenyan got up to get his ringing phone from the living room before returning back to his seat. I tried not to eavesdrop on his call, but it was kind of hard not to. It's not like he was being secretive or anything.

"Hey, how have you been? Yea, I've been back for about two months now. Still trying to get settled. Things have been kind of hectic," he spoke to the caller. "Yea, I'll actually be there tonight. Look forward to seeing you."

I could tell from that the voice on the line belonged to a woman. For some reason, I instantly became jealous and I didn't even know who she was or her relationship with him. There was no reason for me to be thinking some of the thoughts that I was thinking. Kenyan hadn't given me a reason to question him.

"I'm going to get going in a minute and let you get to whatever you need to do today. I had some business that I need to handle. Are you free tonight," he asked after he ended his call.

"Umm, okay. I didn't really have anything planned for later. Probably go over a few designs for this job I have coming up and maybe catch up on my shows. That's it."

"Okay, well I have this charity event I have to attend tonight and I was wondering if you would do me the honor of being my date," he said, clearing our dishes.

"Why wait until the day of to say something, Kenyan?"

"Honestly, baby, it kind of slipped my mind. I meant to bring it up yesterday after I talked to Diane, but I forgot," he told me.

"Well, I don't mind going, but what am I supposed to wear?"

"Don't worry about that, love. Just send me your sizes and I'll have my stylist handle everything," he assured me.

"Your stylist? I don't think I can ever get used to this," I chuckled, getting up from the barstool.

"Well, you better try," he said walking up behind me and smacking me playfully on my bottom. "This is your life now."

"Oh, yea?"

"Yep, and it's not up for debate," he said, planting a kiss on my lips. "I'm going to hop in the shower before I run. Come get in with me."

"No, baby," I giggled and pulled away from him. "You know if I get in there with you, we both won't be getting anything accomplished today."

He stood there contemplating what I said, before a smile broke out on his face. "True. Maybe I should shower alone."

It didn't take long for Kenyan to finish getting ready. He had a packed schedule today and couldn't risk being late all because he wanted to be fresh. I had only met his publicist/manager twice, but I could tell she didn't play any games. I loved her though. Ms. Diane was in her mid-forties and was sort of like another mother figure or an older aunt. She was great at what she did and other than Kenyan's mom, she was a big part of his success. Ms. Diane made sure he kept his head on straight and didn't lose focus like so many young men in his position did.

I glanced at the clock and realized that I had enough time to soak in a warm bath before I needed to meet my mom for lunch. After I was settled in the steamy water, I grabbed my phone so that I could call Morgan.

"Heeeeyyyy, best friend," she answered.

I laughed. "Why must you be so extra?"

"Because extra is my middle name and I wouldn't be me if I wasn't," she laughed along. "What happened after I dropped you off last night? I know Kenyan came over because I passed him when I was leaving."

"Well wouldn't you like to know," I teased.

"Dana Michelle Barnett, do not play with me. I've been waiting for what seems like forever and I know you have some tea for me, so spill. How was it? Still good like you remembered," she questioned anxiously.

My head dropped back to the edge of the tub as my eyes drifted closed, reminiscing about the night before. Or shall I say morning.

"Better than I remembered, Morg," I revealed.

"Oh my god! Better? Come on, Dee. I want details and don't leave anything out."

"I don't even know where to start. You've heard the stories before, but this was soooo different. Kenyan has grown and matured in every sense. The things he did to my body should be illegal. I don't think I've ever experienced anything like what that man did to me last night," I told her.

"Awww. He put it on you, best friend. Got you over there swooning and stuff. Damn, you got me over here feeling some type of way," she said. "Lawd, where is my husband at?"

"I'm not about to play with you," I laughed.

"Who's playing? I'm dead serious right now. You know my horny ass stay on go and that right there just took me there."

"TMI, Morg. TMI," I told her.

"Whatever. But seriously, Dana. I'm glad you quit playing with him. You needed that. Bad."

"Oh, whatever, heifer. Don't do me."

"Nah, I'll leave that to Kenyan."

"You know what? Bye. I'll talk to your crazy tail later," I laughed before we both ended the call.

After finishing my bath, I got dressed and decided to keep things simple. The sheer yellow blouse I wore was paired with a pair of light denim boyfriend jeans and navy booties. Nothing too extravagant.

I had missed the last two lunch dates that my mom and I had planned because I had started to take on clients and things were really hectic right now with the holiday season being right around the corner. I wasn't complaining though. The work was appreciated, as well as those nice checks that came with it.

"So, you two are really giving this a go," my mom asked after I told her about Kenyan and I making things official.

"Yea, we are."

"I'm glad," she smiled. "But listen, Dana. If you're going to do this, put your all into it. You can't let mistakes from the past dictate the future. You both were young and had a lot of learning and growing to do. Move on from that and be happy," my mother advised.

For some reason, I got the feeling that there was more that she wanted to say. Like she might have known something, but didn't want it to be known that she knew. Maybe I was just reading too much into things.

"I'm trying, mama. There are just some things that are kind of hard to overlook," I said, taking a sip of my lemonade. "This isn't the same Kenyan here. He's a freaking celebrity now. It's still crazy to me how people are all over him when we go out. Oh, and don't get me started on the paparazzi. They're insane!"

"Oh, sweetie, I know. Your father and I caught your debut on TMZ," my mom smirked.

"See what I'm talking about? Kenyan tries to tell me that I'll get used to it and learn to ignore them, but I don't think I'll ever get used to that."

"Well, if you love him like I know you do, you'll find a way to make it work."

"Whoa," I said, stopping her. "Love? We're still fresh, mama. I don't think we're quite at love yet."

"Child, please," she shooed me. "You loved him then and you love him now. Those feelings don't just disappear, so tell that mess to someone who doesn't know any better. Now, tell me about this charity thing you two are going to."

I had to shake my head at her. This woman was a trip, but she was right. That love didn't go away. No matter how hard I tried to force it to, it had always been there. Now, with Kenyan back, I'm almost definite it wasn't going anywhere and I was okay with that. My feelings were amplified now. I thought he was irresistible back then, but now? Lord, now, I don't even know what word to use to describe him. He was everything.

I was in love with Kenyan and the man he'd become. Who wouldn't be? However, that right there was one of the biggest problems I found myself facing.

If I saw how amazing Kenyan was, I'm sure all these other women did as well. Hell, his amazingness was spread all over magazine covers, billboards, and anything else you could think of. I knew I was probably just being a little insecure, but I couldn't help it. If you could just see how women threw themselves at him. It didn't matter if I was right there on his arm, they still tried to shoot their shot. One thing I can say, however, was that Kenyan never hesitated to set them straight. He was very big on respect and didn't tolerate disrespect at all. Especially not towards me.

We finished up with lunch and our conversation with the promise of seeing each other Sunday at church. I had been slacking lately and needed to go better with my attendance. I would probably see if I could get Kenyan to join us if this wasn't one of the weekends he went with his family.

"Hello," I said, answering my ringing phone as I got into my car.

"Hey, love," Kenyan's deep voice vibrated through my phone. "How was lunch with moms?"

"It was great. I'm actually just leaving and about to head by the bookstore."

"You mind holding off on the bookstore?"

"Why? What's that," I questioned.

"I have a team that's headed to your place to help you get ready for tonight."

"A team? Kenyan, I don't need a group pf strangers to help me get ready. I'm pretty sure I can manage."

"Baby, I know that, but I don't want you to have to worry about anything. This was already last minute and that's my fault. Just let them come pamper you. Please," he begged. "For me."

"I guess, Kenyan. What time will you be at my place?"

"Actually, I'm going to have a car bring you to the venue and meet me there. I won't be finished up in time to make it to your place," he informed me.

"Ugh. Really, babe?"

"I know, baby. I'm sorry, but I'll make it up to you. I promise."

"You better," I pouted. "I guess I'll see you later."

When I arrived to my townhouse, there was already a truck parked out front, waiting for me. I greeted them and let them enter. This was too much. I mean, there was a hairstylist, makeup artist, nail technician, and the stylist and her two assistants. Like what in the world did I need all of this for?

"I've put together a few selections for you to choose from," the stylist, Carin, told me after I was finished with hair and makeup.

"Okay," I nodded. "What will Kenyan be wearing?"

She smiled and nudged me in the direction of my bedroom. "Don't worry, sweetie. I made sure all of your choices compliment Mr. Spencer's tux perfectly."

"Thank you."

Entering my bedroom, I took in the gorgeous evening gowns that Carin had put out for me. I was immediately drawn to the deep burgundy, off the shoulder gown with a sweetheart neckline. I just had to try that one on first.

You guys wouldn't believe how perfect this dress fit my body. This was the one. I didn't need to try on anything else. I don't think any of the other dresses could top this, and if they could, I'm sure my heart wouldn't be able to handle that.

"Oh, goody! I was hoping you chose that one," Carin clapped. "You look amazing. That dress looks like it was made for you. Kenyan won't be able to keep his eyes off you."

The car that Kenyan sent had arrived and a wave of anxiety washed over me. I had put together a lot of high-class events like this, but this was the first time that I wouldn't be in the background making sure that everything went smoothly. This time I would be in the mist of everything and had to mingle with these people.

Before I knew it, the car was pulling up to our destination and there were people everywhere. I could see some being interviewed on the red carpet, while others posed for pictures. Cameras were everywhere. They were turned towards the truck before we even came to a complete stop. The bright lights from the flashed were blinding and hard to see through.

The back door opened and there stood Kenyan, in all of his handsome glory. He was breathtaking. I meant that literally, too. I could barely draw breath as I sat there staring at him. Damn. I was going to need a change of panties before the night was over with.

# Chapter 10: Kenyan

Stunning. Simple stunning. That was the only way I could describe Dana right now. She was wearing the hell out of that dress and I hadn't even gotten the chance to get a good look at it yet. She was still seated in the back of the truck looking like she was seconds away from ravishing me.

"Do you plan on sitting there or are you going to join me," I chuckled as I extended my hand out to help her.

She smiled shyly and accepted my hand. Once she was on her feet in front of me, I assisted her with smoothing her dress down before closing the truck door.

"Shall we," I asked, as I waited for her to take hold of my arm.

"Kenyan! Over here, Kenyan!"

"Who's the lucky lady?"

"Who is she, Kenyan?"

"Kenyan!"

If there was anything I hated about being in the spotlight, this was it. The paps were relentless. They didn't even give us the chance to breath, let alone answer one of the million questions they were throwing my way. I hadn't really had the opportunity to prepare Dana for what I knew would happen. This hadn't been the first time they've seen Dana on my arm. However, it was the first that they've seen me with the same woman consistently.

I had already made my appearance on the red carpet before Dana had arrived, so I didn't bother to stop when the reporters began throwing questions my way regarding Dana as we posed for pictures. Once we were done, I guided her up the staircase and inside.

"I think I need a drink after that," Dana said.

"Sorry about that, love. I should have warned you about how crazy it was going to be," I apologized while kissing her temple.

There were staff stationed throughout the area with trays of champagne. I stopped one of them and grabbed Dana and myself a flute. I saw a few of my former teammates and headed in their direction.

"My man, Kenyan," Derrick greeted me.

"How've you been, man," I returned, before turning to his wife. "Gwen, you're looking beautiful as always."

"Thank you, Kenyan. It's feels like forever since we've seen you. You just left us hanging," Gwen said, coming to hug me.

"You know it wasn't like that and it's only been a few months. But hey, I have someone I want you two to meet," I said, taking Dana's hand in mine. "Guys this is, Dana. Dana, this is my boy Derrick. We played together in Miami. And this beauty here is his lovely wife, Gwen."

"It's nice to meet you two," Dana said shaking both of their hands.

"Oh, honey, it's a pleasure," Gwen smiled and cut her eyes at me, with a knowing look.

I already knew what she was thinking. I'm sure it was the same thing that everyone else was. They were trying to figure out exactly what Dana was to me. I had no problem screaming to the gods that she was my woman, but whose business was that?

"Babe," Dana called to me. "Where are the restrooms?"

"They're right over there," I directed her. "I'll be over here when you're done."

My eyes followed the sway of her hips until she was no longer in my line of sight. It had barely been ten seconds and I was already missing her. I shook my head and laughed inwardly. Look at me. I was already acting like some sprung, love-sick teen. Who cares, though? Dana was my woman and I could ogle at her all I wanted.

"Look at you," Gwen said, approaching my side. "If I didn't know any better, I would think you were in love."

"Well, would you look at who we have here," a voice spoke from behind us.

I knew that high-pitched voice from anywhere. Even though I was dreading turning around, I did so anyway. As annoyed with her presence as I was, I couldn't deny that she looked great in her strapless, emerald evening gown. It complimented her smooth chocolate skin perfectly.

"How've you been, Kenyan," Missy said, coming to place a lingering kiss on my cheek. "I haven't spoken to you since you moved back out here. I've missed you."

"I've been great, Missy," I said, stepping back to put some distance between us.

I chose not to even address her comment about missing me. That was BS. She only missed the perks of being associated with me. Missy and I had a consistent casual thing going on. She was always a call away when I need to relieve "stress" and she'd had no problem accompanying me whenever I had an impromptu event and needed a date. I would hit her off with a few dollars here and there, but that was about it. No expensive shopping trips or extravagant getaways like she thought she was going to get from me.

"I'm glad to hear that."

Gwen was still standing to the side of me and she made no attempt at hiding the displeased look on her face. Gwen was very familiar with Missy and to say that she wasn't a fan of hers would be an understatement. Missy was one of those women who were just looking for a come up or some type of notoriety.

"Oh, I almost didn't notice you standing there, Gwen," Missy remarked, snidely.

"I bet."

"Be nice," I whispered, before kissing Gwen on the forehead.

"Okay, I'm ready," Dana approached, snapping her clutch closed.. "Hope I didn't have you guys waiting too long."

"Of course not," I responded, pulling her into my side.

Missy still stood in front of us, now eyeing Dana like she was the one intruding.

"Are you going to introduce me to your friend, Kenyan," Missy asked.

"Oh, hi," Dana said, extending her hand to Missy. "I'm Dana. His girlfriend."

"Girlfriend?"

"Yes. I'm sorry, but I still didn't get your name."

"Is she serious, Kenyan? So, she's your woman? Since when? Because I don't recall her being your woman when-."

"Isn't that what she just told you, Missy? I tried being cordial, but you sitting here questioning me like you have the right to isn't cool," I told her. "What you just did was very disrespectful to myself and Dana, which you know I don't tolerate. Have a little dignity and walk away now, before I forget we're at this nice event."

Dana placed her hand gently on my bicep to calm me. "Relax, babe. I'm sure she was just caught off guard and didn't know any better. Hopefully this won't be an issue again. Let's go find our seats."

"I knew I liked you," Gwen snickered, looping her arm through Dana's and heading in the direction of our assigned table. "So nice-nasty with it."

"You've got a feisty one on your hands," Derrick chuckled as we followed behind the ladies, leaving Missy behind.

"Don't I know it," I said, licking my lips as I watched Dana.

****

"Oh, man. I don't remember the last time I've had one of these bad boys," I said, taking a bite of the juicy burger and sitting it back in its container.

We had just finished dinner at the charity gala not even two hours ago and were sitting here on my living room floor, stuffing our faces. Another thing I loved above Dana. She wasn't afraid to chow down in front of me like most women. That dainty little food they called themselves serving us at the gala did nothing for us. The attendees were made up of probably sixty percent athletes and they couldn't come up with a more fitting menu? We were big men with big appetites.

"Did you enjoy yourself tonight," I asked Dana.

"Yes, I actually did," she said, stuffing her face full of loaded cheese fries. "Other than your little boo-thing shooting daggers at me all night."

Wiping my mouth with a napkin, I eyed her to try to read her expression. That was hard considering the fact that she had her eyes trained on her food and avoiding my gaze. I didn't know if she was upset about the Missy situation or not.

"She's not my boo thing, love. Just someone I would fool with from time to time. I wasn't even in contact with her before I moved back," I explained.

"Kenyan, you don't have to explain yourself to me. You-."

"Yes, I do have to explain myself and always will when I feel it's necessary," I stopped her. "I never want there to be any doubt in your mind when it comes to us and your place in my life. When it comes to you, I'm an open book, baby girl."

Moving my now empty container to the side, I grabbed hold to one of Dana's ankle and tugged her towards me. Giggling, she tried her best to free herself from me and get away.

"Stop, Ken," she laughed.

"You don't tell me to stop, woman."

"Says who," she sassed.

"Our relationship contract."

"Relationship contract? You must've bumped your head getting out the car tonight."

"Nope, I didn't and right on page ten, paragraph two, it clearly states that you can't tell me no, stop, or anything of that nature," I said, nibbling on her neck as I spoke.

"I must have skipped that page," she moaned.

"Must have," I said.

Gently laying her back on the plush rug that covered my hard-wood floors, I hovered above her and marvelled in her beauty. In my eyes, Dana was perfect. I don't think I could say that enough. The confidence that radiated from her pores as my eyes began to roam her body, was one of the biggest turn-ons.

"Damn, you're beautiful."

Dana blushed and wrapped her arms under my shoulders to pull me closer to her. "You know you tell me that at least a hundred times a day, right?"

"Only a hundred? Dang, I need to step my game up," I said, pulling her bottom lip into my mouth.

With mesmerized eyes, Dana laid there staring at me. I could see the wheels turning in her head.

"What's wrong, love?"

"Oh, nothing's wrong. Actually everything's perfect. Almost too perfect," she told me.

"Nothing's ever perfect, baby girl, but I strive to make it as close to perfection as I can," I said.

"Are you running game on me Mr. Spencer," Dana smirked, teasingly.

"Trust me. I don't need to run game," I said, playfully smacking her thigh. "I already have you where I want you."

"Yea? And where is that?"

"Falling."

Her expression grew serious and she shied away from my gaze. That was a reoccurring thing with Dana. Any time I brought up a subject that she didn't want to address, she would shrink away from me. I planned on nipping that in the bud early. I needed her to be as open with me as I was with her.

"Hey," I said, placing my hand under her chin to turn her focus back to me. "Don't be trying to get all shy on me now."

"I'm not."

"Then what do you call it, because it loo-."

The ringing of both my phones interrupted what I was about to say. I asked Dana to give me a moment so that I could answer, since I figured it must have been important if both of my lines were going off.

"What's going on, Ms. Di," I greeted after realizing that it was my manager calling my personal line.

For Diane to be calling my phone at damn near two in the morning, it had to be something. However, I was nowhere near prepared for what came out of her mouth next.

# Chapter 11: Dana

To say that Kenyan was pissed would be an understatement. I don't think I had ever seen this man this upset. As a matter of fact, I don't believe I've ever witnessed him angry at all. But right about now? Right about now he was fuming. He stood in front of me yelling into his phone, while he paced back and forth like a madman. I had long ago lost count of the many curse words that left his mouth. I knew it had to be something big.

"Where the hell is this shit coming from? I need this handled, Diane! ASAP!"

He never spoke to her like that. Never! Ms. Diane wasn't even the type to tolerate it. I was really curious to know what was going on but I figured it would be best if I let him tell me once he calmed down. That's only if it was something he wanted me to know.

I got up from the floor to leave the room so that I could give him some privacy. He was so into his conversation that he seemed to not even notice my departure. Since he was tied up right now, I decided to hop in the shower and clean myself of today's events.

After about a good twenty minutes of being in the shower, I cut the water off and wrapped myself in a towel. I quickly lotioned up and threw on one of Kenyan's oversized shirt, before leaving to search for him. Things were quiet now and he could no longer be heard yelling obscenities into his phone. I checked his living room and then his man cave, but came up empty. I figured he must have left and I was about to head back upstairs to his bedroom until I noticed the notification light blinking on my phone.

I grabbed it from the counter as I was passing and checked my phone as I walked up the stairs. A few of them were from Facebook and Instagram, both of which I rarely ever used if it wasn't pertaining to my business accounts. I bypassed those and went to the messages from Morgan. The fact that she had written in all caps was the first indicator that something was up. I hurried to call her so that I could make sure that she and my god-babies were okay.

"What's going on, Morg? Why are you texting me 911?"

"That's what I'm trying to figure out, Dana. What the hell is going on? Where's Kenyan?"

"Wait. Kenyan? What does Kenyan have to do with anything? What the hell is going on," I asked, now nervous.

Something was definitely up. First, Kenyan gets that call in the middle of the night that sent him into a rampage and now Morgan on my phone in a panic, asking me where he is. Somebody had better start telling me something.

"What rock have you been living under, Dana? You've been plastered all over almost every gossip site and media outlet for the last few hours. They're going crazy," Morgan explained.

"For what? Is all of this because of the charity event? There were a few paparrazi there, so I'm sure they couldn't wait to report spotting me and Kenyan together. It's not that deep."

"Forget that damn charity thing. We're talking about some heifer running to the media dragging you and Kenyan through the mud. She claims that she and Kenyan were in a relationship and he disappeared and never returned. Said that he was cheating on her with you. Calling you all types of home-wreckers."

"What," I shrieked.

"Exactly," Morgan said. "She's even telling these people that this man was abusing her and that she was pregnant and-."

"PREGNANT?!"

There is no way this could be happening right now. I just knew things were too good to be true. All that smooth talking his ass did and I fell right into his trap. I was about to find him and give him a piece of my mind. He may have only known the sweet Dana, but Mr. Kenyan Spencer was about to see a whole other side of me today.

"Morgan, I'll call you back," I said and hung up before she could respond.

I dialed Kenyan's cell so that I wouldn't have to go searching through this big ass house for him again. I didn't have the time nor patience for that.

"Where are you," I demanded as soon as he picked up the phone.

"On the patio," he answered, with stress evident in his voice. "Dana-."

I hung up before he could say anything else. I didn't want him talk now. He could do all the talking he needed to do once we were standing face to face.

I made it downstairs and to the kitchen where the door to the patio was located. I swung the door open and stalked over to where Kenyan was sitting, with a pretty big glass of brown liquor. He noticed the expression on my face and quickly stood.

"Baby-."

I threw my hand up to stop him. "When did you plan on saying something to me, Kenyan? You don't think I had the right to know," I yelled at him.

"Dana, lower your voice and calm down. If you want to talk, fine, but you're not about to be standing here yelling at me like I'm some child."

"Don't you tell me to calm down. I have every right not to be calm right now," I snapped. "Is this serious, Kenyan? Who is this woman and what the hell is she talking about?"

Kenyan ran both of his palms down his face and released a heavy sigh. I don't care how irritated he seemed to be. He'd better get to explaining and quick. He resumed his position back in his seat and motioned for me to join him.

"No, I'd rather stand," I declined.

"Really, Dana? Sit down," he said. "Please."

Huffing, I moved to take a seat, but made sure to put enough distance between us.

"Okay. I'm listening."

"Look, I'm not sure how much you've seen and heard on your own, but you already know that there were plenty paps at the event tonight. I'm assuming after those pictures got out there, it upset a few people. One of them being a chick that I used to fool around with."

"So, all of this behind someone you were boning in the past?"

"Not exactly."

"What the hell does not exactly mean, Kenyan? Now is not the time for you to be talking in circles."

"Me and the woman had some heavy dealings, but the chick turned out to be bat-shit crazy, so I cut her off. She would pop up at my condo, at practices. Her crazy ass was convinced that we were destined to be because she had dreams about it," he said, shaking his head. "Man, at one point this woman was actually telling people that we were engaged. Luckily, that rumor didn't get too far. Baby, everything out that woman's mouth has been a lie. Why wait until I go public with my relationship to try to put all this out and bad-mouth me? She just wants attention and I refuse to give it to her."

"So, all of this is a lie? Even the whole pregnancy thing?"

"Bullshit. All bullshit. Ain't no way in hell that woman is or ever has been pregnant by me."

"This can't be happening. Who in their right mind would even do something like this?"

"That's the point. She's not in her right mind," Kenyan told me and took one of my hands into his. "But I'm handling it, baby. I'm sorry you even have to deal with this mess."

I relaxed a little and allowed him to pull me closer so that I was laying on his chest. I don't know why I even allowed myself to get so worked up. That wasn't even Kenyan. The things that this woman was spreading weren't even close to believable.

"What do we do now," I questioned.

"Well, you don't do anything. Let me handle this, love. I don't want you stressing about this, Dana. This will be over and behind us before you know it."

"Are you sure, Kenyan. I'm not cut out for all this."

He turned my body so that I was facing him. "Do you trust me, Dana?"

"Of course."

"Then trust me when I say I got this. There's nothing for you to worry about," he assured me.

I removed myself from his arms and stood to my feet. "Come on. It's time to go to bed. All of this mess has me tired and I need special attention."

"Yes ma'am."

\*\*\*\*

"Uncle Ken!"

As soon as we entered his parents' home, his niece Karli come rushing in our direction. She was the perfect mix of Kendrick and Charli.

"Come here, Uncle Ken. I have to show you something," she beamed, while tugging at his arm.

"Whoa there, baby girl. Let us get in the door," he laughed. "Aren't you going to say hi to Dana?"

"Hi, Dana. You can see, too," she said, grabbing both of our hands and pulling us to follow her.

Her energy was contagious. Along with that radiant smile of hers. Karli was downright adorable.

"Look," she instructed, pulling us over to the kitchen counter so we could have a look at the cookies she'd been decorating.

"These look great. Did you do this all on your own," Kenyan asked as he lifted her into his arms.

"Nana helped," she told him. "They're for you."

"Thank you, but that's a lot of cookies. Are you going to help me eat them?"

"Yes," she eagerly answered. "Ms. Dana, too."

"And what about your Nana who helped you make all of these cookies," his mother asked, entering the kitchen. "Hey babies. How are y'all?"

"Hey, mama," Kenyan said, going over and kissing her cheek. "Where's everybody at?"

"Your sister's upstairs and everyone else is in the family room. You know your dad and brother are glued to that TV. Charli's in there with them. I don't see how she can stand all that yelling," she said. "Hey, Dana baby."

"Hi, Mrs. Spencer."

"Child if I have to tell you one more time about that," she chastised.

"I know, mama. I'm sorry."

She came over and ushered me out of the room so we could have some privacy, leaving Kenyan and Karli in the kitchen to feast on cookies.

"Are you okay," she questioned once we were alone.

I sighed. "I'm trying to be."

"How are you really feeling though, sweetie," she asked, concern lacing her voice.

"I want to stay positive, but it's hard," I confessed. "The things that these people have been saying is ridiculous. They don't even know me and my name is being dogged. I told Kenyan that I would be patient and let him handle it, but this is starting to affect my work. I haven't even been to my office this week because it's surrounded by paparazzi."

"This is the first time that Kenyan has ever been caught up in a scandal, so I know it must be tough. The media has been waiting for the opportunity to get some dirt on my baby."

"But why though? Everyone loves Kenyan."

"And that's exactly why. The only thing they care about is getting a juicy story. Kenyan's pretty private and there really isn't much of anything negative they can find on him. The most someone can say is that he's been seen with a few women over the years, so they assume he's a playboy," she spoke. "I've told that child about dealing with these scandalous women. Just nothing but trouble. Oh, and STD's. Trouble and a whole lot of STD's."

I couldn't contain the laugh that escaped my mouth. What was I going to do with this woman? But she was right. It's sad to say, but a majority of woman nowadays were trouble. Even though all of this was new to me, I didn't plan on walking away. I guess this was a test on how strong Kenyan and I's foundation truly was.

"Hey, Dana," Kelsey greeted, bouncing into the room.

"Hey, Kelsey. You're might chipper today. Who are you all dressed up for?"

"Her little boo," Mrs. Spencer answered before she could. "He's joining us this evening for dinner."

"Uh oh. I see why Kenyan made sure we were on time today. You nervous," I asked her.

"Why would I be? Kenyan doesn't scare anybody," Kelsey replied defiantly.

"Oh, I don't? Well we'll see when this lil' punk gets here," Kenyan spoke, sneaking up behind us.

"Whatever, Kenny. This is exactly why I haven't introduced you two yet. Don't go trying to run him off,' Kelsey begged. "You already be having people about to piss their pants with how huge you are."

"So what? This your way of warning me that your boyfriend's a wuss and will be intimidated by my size?"

"Kenyan," Kelsey whined.

"Don't worry, Kels. He'll be on his best behavior," I promised her.

"Says who," Kenyan shot with a raised brow.

"Says me. Now behave, Kenyan."

"Whatever. I'll behave, alright. What time is this kid getting here? I'm ready to eat."

"He's not a kid, Kenny," Kelsey sassed. "And neither am I."

She'd might as well save her little "I'm an Adult" speech because Kenyan had already walked off. I was going to do my best to make sure that Kenyan didn't cut up once this boy got here. He had already put it in his head that he was going to give the poor guy a hard time, and once his mind was made up that was pretty much it.

Poor Kelsey. I couldn't imagine what she went through with him. Luckily for her he was already off in Florida around the time she first started dating. However, this was her first serious boyfriend, as well as the first one that Kenyan was getting the chance to meet. I couldn't wait to see how this whole thing goes.

"He's here," Kelsey announced after the doorbell sounded. "Please make sure my brother acts right, Dana."

"I got you, baby girl. Don't worry about him."

"Kelsey, stop stalling and go answer the door," Kenyan yelled from the kitchen. "People ready to eat."

"Ugh! Mama, I really am starting not to like your son," Kelsey fussed as she went to answer the door.

# Chapter 12: Kenyan

"Are we still going to go see the show tonight," Dana asked as she stood in the mirror getting ready.

Even though Dana hadn't been able to spend much time at her office because of the constant harassment from reporters and paparazzi, she was still making the best of everything. Instead of going in, many of her clients had no problem meeting her elsewhere. Dana hadn't said anything yet, but I knew she was about fed up with all the drama. Which is exactly why this trip I was taking today had to happen.

Dana wasn't aware of what I planned on doing today and I planned on keeping it that way. I was almost certain that she wouldn't be okay with it. My lady may have been a sweetheart, but she had a mean streak and trust me when I say you did not want to get on her bad side.

"Yea, we're still going. If starts at eight, so we'll need to leave out around maybe six-thirty. Do you think that'll give you enough time to do what you need to do?"

"There isn't much I'll have to do. Just shower and change. I'm doing finishing touches for the wedding reception today, so I shouldn't have a long day. God-willing, everything will be in order," she said, grabbing her purse and charger from my dresser. "Give me kiss."

"What's the magic word," I teased.

"Now."

I pretended to think on it. "I guess that'll do," I finally responded.

"It better. See you later, baby. I'll call you when I have a free moment."

"Okay, love. I have a few meetings this morning, so if you can't reach me, that's why."

"Okay."

I waited for Dana to leave before I got up to get ready. My flight was set to leave in about two hours so I needed to get a move on it. Hopefully, this wasn't going to take up my entire day. I could come up with a thousand and one things that I would rather be doing.

"Hello," I answered my phone.

"Good morning, Kenyan," Diane greeted me. "Your car should be arriving in twenty minutes."

"Thanks, Di. I'm getting ready to hop in the shower now."

"Why must you do everything at the last minute?"

I laughed because I knew that was one of her pet peeves. "Dana stayed over last night, so I wanted to wait until she left for work."

"So I'm guessing you didn't tell her," she inquired.

"No, I didn't feel like it was necessary. I don't plan on being gone long anyway. After we handle this, hopefully things will go back to normal."

"I hope so, because this entire ordeal has been running me up the wall," she sighed. "But I still feel as though you should have discussed things with Dana. You're going to a whole other state without saying anything to her."

"Di, don't worry about that. I'll handle Dana."

"Yea, if you say so. Go ahead and get yourself together. I don't want to be waiting at this airport for you all day."

"Alright. I'll see you in a few," I told her before disconnecting the call.

The flight was a quick one and we were unloading the plane before we knew it. Since this was a last-minute trip, I didn't have time to charter a private plane. I rarely travelled that way anyway, but I imagine it would have been a lot more peaceful. Everywhere I turned there was someone shoving a camera in my face. That was one of the most annoying things ever. I don't see how I managed to deal with it for this long.

I made sure to pull the hood to my jacket over my head and hide my face behind a pair of oversized sunglasses. The last thing I needed was for more people to recognize me. Diane exited the flight long before I did to make sure that our car was in place. I didn't bring a bag with me, so I bypassed the baggage claim area and headed in the direction that Diane texted me to meet her.

I was almost to the door and in the clear when I heard my name being yelled from behind me. My first mind told me to take off out the door, but before I could move, everyone had begun to look in my direction.

"That is him! It's Kenyan Spencer," a young boy announced excitedly.

Well, there goes my cover. A crowd was quickly starting to form. As much as I loved my fans and supporters, now was not the time. I was trying to get out of here. I had already spotted a few reporters standing around, but now they were headed in my direction just like everyone else.

"Kenyan! Over this way, Kenyan!"

"What are you doing back in Miami?"

"Are the rumors true? Did you cheat on your model fiancé with the woman you were spotted with at the charity event a few weeks ago?"

"Are you here to fix your relationship? Kenyan!"

I continued to ignore them while I signed one more autograph, before rushing from the airport. They weren't letting up, though. They were right on my heels, throwing question after question at me as I maneuvered through the crowd.

"Alright, that's enough. Clear a path so the young man can walk," an elderly gentleman spoke as he pushed a few of the cameras out of my way.

"Thank you," I said, graciously.

He nodded in return and let me get pass him. Times like these I probably should have gotten security. I never was really fond of having security because I felt as though it only drew even more attention my way. It's safe to say that I appreciate them a bit more now.

The driver was standing holding the back door to the car open for me and I could see Diane already seated in the back. I hopped in and breathed a sigh of relief. I was ready to get back to Dallas already and I had only been in Miami a hot second.

"So, I've already given the driver the address that I was able to obtain. You sure you want to go there first," Diane question, skeptically.

"Yes, Di. I'm sure. I'm trying to get all this over with and behind me. No point in drawing it out longer than it has to be."

"Okay, if you say so," Diane said and sat back as the car began to move.

I looked down at my phone and noticed that I had a text message from Dana. A smile instantly found its way onto my face.

*Sweets: Ugh! This woman is driving me crazy! The flower shop sent over the wrong arrangements so now bride is hysterical *sad face**

*Me: LOL. Hang in there, baby. Minor setback. Other than the bride of chucky, how's your morning coming?*

*Sweets: Slowly making it, babe. I'm going to need some EXTRA special attention after today. ;)*

*Me: You know I got you, love.*

*Sweets: Oh, I know and I can't wait. I have to go. TTYL. Love you!!*

Tucking my phone back into my pocket, I laid my head back against the headrest and closed my eyes. I needed to get my mind right so that I didn't lose my temper when we got here. I was usually the level-headed type, but when something really took me there? Let's just say it was better to steer clear and stay out of my way.

"Kenyan," Diane called, tapping my arm. "We're here."

Opening my eyes, I glanced out the window towards the home that we had pulled up in front of. This wasn't where I remembered coming. But then again, I never bothered to pay much attention either.

"You want me to come in with you," Diane asked.

"Nall, I got it."

"Kenyan, I really don't think that's a smart idea. I can wait in another room, but as your publicist and manager, I would advise against going in there alone."

"Diane, I'm a grown man. I think I can handle myself."

"It's not about being able to handle yourself, because I know you're very capable. This is about covering your tracks when it comes to dealing with manipulative people who are already out to get you."

I sighed and rubbed my hand down my face. Something I always did when I was frustrated or stressed.

"Come on, Di," I said before getting out of the car.

After ringing the doorbell, we both stood there waiting for someone to answer. Someone had to be here, because there was a car in the driveway and I could hear music coming from behind the door. I tried the doorbell again.

"Just wait a minute," someone yelled from the other side of the door. "No need to be impatient."

The door opened and a woman stuck her head out. She looked at Diane first, but once she got to me, her eyes bucked and I could tell that she was a bit nervous in my presence. I'm sure the scowl that I was wearing wasn't helping matters either.

"Umm.. You.. You're umm.. You're Kenyan, right," she stuttered.

"Right. Where's Hazel," I said, getting straight to the point of my visit.

"Look, I know she's caused-."

"Listen, I'm really not up for the extra chit-chat. Is she here or not?"

"Yea, she's inside," she answered and slowly opened the door for us.

Diane and I stepped inside and waited for the woman to show us the way. I could tell she was trying to stall because she was walking extremely slow in front of us.

"By the way, I'm Hazel's sister, Blu," she told us.

I didn't say anything. I wasn't really trying to take my anger out on her and be rude, but now was not the time for pleasantries. I couldn't care less if her name was Yellow.

"Hazel," she called out over the music. "Hazel! You have guests."

"Oh, goody. Who's here to see me," Hazel asked excitedly.

I stepped completely in the room with Diane right beside me so that Hazel could have a clear view. She smiled wide and rushed in my direction.

"Baby! I knew you would come back!"

I managed to dodge her attempt at hugging me and stood there looking at her like she was crazy. Had this chick lost her mind? She'd spread lie after lie about me and almost ruined my relationship. Did she really think this was a friendly visit? There must have been a few screws loose up there.

"You're not happy to see me, Kenny Pooh?"

"Hell no and stop calling me that," I snapped. "You need to come clean and stop spreading all these lies, Hazel. This has gone on long enough."

"Lies? What lies? I've done nothing but told these people the truth about their sweet, golden-boy Kenyan," she smirked. "We were happily in love and you just up and left me to be with that tramp that you've been parading around with."

"Are you serious right now," I asked, scratching my head. "You can't be. This has to be some sort of joke. Am I being pranked or something?"

"Our love isn't a joke. How could you just leave me and our baby all alone? I thought you loved us," she said, rubbing her flat stomach as if an actual baby was in there.

"Our baby?! Are you fucking insane? If you are pregnant, which I highly doubt, the thing damn sure ain't mine!"

I could feel my temperature rising and I was two seconds away from grabbing this looney-tune by the throat and choking some sense into her. I mean, the chick was downright delusional. It was like she had actually convinced herself that the things she was saying were true. Diane must have noticed that I was close to blowing up, because she placed her hand on my arm and told me to let her handle it.

"Listen, sweetheart. Either you cut the BS and tell the truth or you're going to have a lawsuit on your hands for defamation. Now, we want to handle this without having to get the courts involved, but know that our lawyers are already on standby," Diane informed her.

"Do what you have to do. Kenyan and I's love is strong enough to conquer all," Hazel told her.

Blu grabbed her arm and swung her around to face her.

"Hazel, stop this now. This man does not love you. Do you not understand that the shit you're doing is messing with people's lives?"

"Shut up, Blu! You don't know what you're talking about! Kenyan does love me and we're getting married," Hazel yelled at her sister. "Isn't that right, Kenyan?"

"This was a complete waste of time," I said, shaking my head. "You'll be hearing from my lawyers, Hazel."

I told Diane that we were leaving and began heading for the door. Blu was saying something to me, but I didn't want to hear that. Obviously, Hazel really was out of her mind. If Blu really cared about her sister, she would take her somewhere to seek professional help.

"Kenyan, please don't leave! I can fix us some dinner and we can work on fixing our relationship," Hazel pleaded after I'd opened the door. "Why are you doing this to me? You told me you loved me!"

"That's bullshit, Hazel," I barked. "I never told you I loved you! NEVER! That's just some dumbass fairy-tale that you made up in that twisted ass brain of yours!"

Hazel was now on her knees, holding onto my leg like a little kid. That only pissed me off even more. I snatched my leg away from her grasp and stepped onto the porch.

"Oh, God. Kenyan," Diane spoke in a hushed tone.

"What," I snapped, unintentionally at her.

I had barely turned completely in her direction when what seemed like a thousand lights began flashing in my direction. I head snapped back in Hazel's direction and I swear I wanted to knock that stupid smirk right off her face. I've never felt such a strong urge to lay hands on a woman. My parents didn't raise me that way, but I'm sure this would be that one exception.

"We need to get out of here now," Diane said and grabbed my arm.

"Kenyan! Kenyan!"

"What are you doing at Hazel's home? Didn't you say there was nothing going on with you two?"

"You seemed pretty aggressive with her! Are the abuse rumors true?"

"Kenyan!"

We made it into the back and the car and ordered the driver to hurry and get away from there. I just knew the press was about to have a field day with this. Why the hell did I come here in the first place? I should have just proceeded with the lawsuit. But no, I had to try to give her a chance to come clean without getting the courts involved. Stupid! This woman was about to destroy everything I worked so hard to build.

"Fuck," I yelled, hitting the seat in front of me.

# Chapter 13: Dana

Kenyan had been acting strange all week. Something was off with him. I could feel it. I'd been around him enough to learn his moods and I must say, I wasn't feeling this new one he was in. I planned on bringing it up later when he came over. Right now I was about to enjoy my day and I would deal with Kenyan later.

"She's so beautiful," I swooned as I held baby Kendra.

Charli had given birth earlier this week and today was their first day home. Kendrick had made a big deal about not wanting another girl, but you wouldn't know that with how he'd been acting.

He barely gave anyone the chance to hold her, because she was always in his arms. Luckily for me, he had left out the pick up some food. Kendra was just so adorable and looked just like Kendrick. The only thing Charli did was carry her because she was her father's clone.

"My sister's pretty just like me," Karli beamed while playing with her little fingers.

"She sure is," I agreed.

"Mommy let me feed her, too. I'm a good big sister," she bragged.

"You sure are, baby," Charli told her. "Can you go and get mommy a bottle of water from the fridge?"

"Yes, mommy," she said eagerly and bounced from the room.

"I see she's quite the little helper."

"She really is. Kendrick and I thought that it would take her longer to adjust. She's been the only child for so long and spoiled rotten, but she really loves being a big sister. Her little butt barely wants Kendrick and I to do anything. Even if Kendra cries, Karli's jumping up before us to see what's wrong," she laughed.

Karli came back in the room with two water bottles and handed one to both her mother and me.

"Mommy, can I watch Frozen while my sister is sleeping?"

"Of course, baby. I'll be right back, Dana. You can just put the baby in the crib if you want," Charli told me, before going to set Karli up on the TV.

I really didn't want to put the baby down, but I figured she would be more comfortable in her crib. After making sure her blanket was secure around her, I stood looking down at her as she slept. She was so tiny and perfect. I could probably stand here forever looking at her. She was sleeping so peacefully, without a care in the world.

"Hard to take your eyes off her, ain't it," Charli asked, coming to stand because me.

"It really is."

"I know. I be sneaking in here in the middle of the night just to watch her sleep," she smiled down at Kendra.

She turned on the baby monitor and we both left out of the nursery and went to the living room.

"How's everything going," Charli asked after we both got settled on the couch.

"It's going," I sighed.

"Nuh uh. What's wrong? Talk to me," Charli urged.

"Something's up with Kenyan. He's been acting really strange these last few days. Anytime I ask what's wrong, he always says nothing and changes the subject," I confided.

"Maybe it's just everything with that woman Hazel that's got him acting different. That would stress anyone out," Charli said.

"Yea, but I don't think that's quite it. That whole thing has been going on for a minute now and he didn't start acting like this until recently."

"I'm sure it's nothing, Dana," she tried to assure me. "Don't stress yourself about it. Just be there for him when he's ready to talk about it. That's all I can tell you."

"Yea, I guess."

"Are you guys still planning on making it to the couples' trip that Morgan and Rich planned?"

"Yea, we're still going. We need that vacation more than anything right about now."

"I wish Kendrick and I could go, but that's out of the question. I know Kendrick's not having that," she chuckled.

"You're right about that," I laughed along with her. "Don't worry. We'll just have to plan another one when the baby's maybe a few months and Kendrick isn't being the overprotective papa bear."

"You're right about that. When do you think you and Kenyan will start on a few of your own?"

"Umm," I gulped.

My throat had suddenly become dry. I wasn't quite expecting that question. Of course the thought had crossed my mind, but it never stayed for long. That wasn't something I even wanted to think about. Just... No.

"Umm. Kenyan and I hadn't discussed children. I mean, we're still fresh. I don't think having kids is on either of our radars right now," I answered as best as I could.

"Oh, wow," she said and sat back. "I'm sorry. I just assumed that was something you guys had talked about. I know that Kenyan wants a big family and that's all he and his brother have been talking about."

"What," I questioned nervously.

"You know what," she said. "How about we scrap this convo hun? It's really not any of my business anyway."

I was thankful that her phone started to ring and she got up to take the call. That was a conversation that I wasn't ready to have. I could feel an anxiety attack creeping up every time conversation seemed to go in that direction, which was often when I was around Mrs. Spencer or my mother. If it was up to those two, I would already be on baby number three.

I heard the garage door open and close and knew that Kendrick had returned.

"Hey, Dee. I didn't know you were still here," Kendrick said, coming to kiss me on the cheek. "Where's Charls?"

"She had to take a call."

"Oh, okay. I got Chinese food. You want some," he offered.

"Thanks, but I'm okay. I'm about to get out of here anyway. I need to run to the grocery store before it gets too late," I told him.

"Okay. Be careful out there," he said, sounding like his brother.

I laughed and shook my head. "How careful do I need to be just to go to the store," I joked.

"Very," he laughed. "Too many crazy people out here. Don't act like can't nobody snatch your little behind up."

"They'll have a hard time trying."

"Okay, tough guy. Just be safe."

"Hey, baby. I didn't know you were back," Charli said, coming to deliver a kiss to his lips. "You leaving, Dana?"

"Yea, I need to be getting out of here. I call you later."

"Okay, girl. Be careful."

\*\*\*\*

"Kenyan, baby. Oh god," I moaned out as I tried to handle everything he was giving me.

"How does that feel, baby? Tell me how good I'm making your body feel," he urged as he dipped deeper into my honey pot.

"It's feels soooo good, baby. Please don't stop! I'm about to cum!"

"Don't worry, love. I don't plan on stopping. Let it all out for me," he groaned while biting down on my shoulder. "Shit, sweets. You feel so damn good, baby."

Kenyan's voice always sent me over the edge. It didn't matter how hard I tried to tune him out, the sweet nothings he would whisper in my ear seemed to arouse me more. Oh, and the biting. Lord, the biting! That was one of my weaknesses.

I threw my head back into the pillow as my mouth dropped open. A wave so strong hit my body and left me floating on clouds. My body was still trying to recover when Kenyan turned me on my side and placed my leg on his shoulder. He knew I couldn't take this position! I felt all of him like this. ALL OF HIM!

"Kenyan! Baby, hold on. God, you're so deep. Wait, baby," I pleaded, as I placed my hand against his pelvis to try to stop him.

"Move your hand, sweets."

"Baby, you-."

"Move your hand."

Doing what I was told, I moved my hand and grabbed the comforter. He was stroking me with such expertise that I could feel another orgasm swiftly approaching. I didn't think my body could handle another one.

"I'm about to cum, sweets. Cum with me, love."

"I'm there, baby. Oh, god I'm there!"

We both released at the same time and rode our orgasms together. Instead of pulling out, Kenyan lowered my leg and pushed deeper inside of me, before pulling the covers over us.

"Umm, baby," I called out weakly because my voice was almost gone from all the screaming I was doing.

"Yea," he replied lazily.

"Aren't you going to move?"

"Eventually."

"Eventually? Really, Kenyan," I asked, hitting his shoulder.

"Yes, really. Just let me take a quick nap."

"Baby, you're too big. You're going to squish me," I whined.

Huffing, he adjusted myself and shifted his weight so that it wasn't all resting on me.

"There. Better?"

"Yea, Kenyan," I said, shaking my head at how spoil he was.

I decided to take a nap with him since it looked as though I wasn't going to be able to move any time soon. I was tired anyway. Going four rounds back-to-back with Kenyan would do that to you. I'm not sure where this man got his stamina from. It's like he would downed a case of RedBull or something.

I didn't realize exactly how tired I was until I woke up three hours later, in bed alone. Looking around the room, I noticed that Kenyan had straightened up the mess we'd made. We'd been in such a rush to get to each other that we'd just discarded our clothes all over the place. I was still feeling the effects from our love-making session and wanted nothing more than to sleep the rest of the day away. However, since Kenyan and I both were huge procrastinators, we hadn't packed anything at all for our trip. A trip in which we were set to leave for in about ummm... Four hours!

Standing up from the bed, I stretched my aching limps and went into the bathroom to take a quick shower. I didn't have time to drag my feet. We were working on a very tight time schedule. I hurried through my shower and decided to dress comfortably for our flight. Dressed in a pair of tights, comfy sweater, and my favorite pair of riding boots, I went to search for Kenyan. He couldn't be too far because I could hear his voice carrying through the halls.

"Baby," I called out. "Where are you?"

He didn't respond so I figured wherever he was, he couldn't hear me. I heard the sound of his TV playing in his office and went to check to see if that's where he was.

I found him bent over his desk, typing away on his computer with his phone glued to his ear. He hadn't noticed me standing in the doorway and I hadn't planned on eavesdropping until something on the TV caught my attention and caused my ears to perk up. I propped my hands on my hips and looked at him. He finally looked up from the computer screen and I noticed the nervous expression on his faced. Yea, he was in trouble and he knew it.

"Okay, baby. I can explain that," he said before I could even open my mouth.

"I'm listening."

He sighed before muting the television. "All of that happened after I went down to Miami to try to straighten all this mess out. Instead of things going smoothly, like I had hoped, she was completely out of her mind. Like delusional."

"Yea, I got that part, but what I'm still trying to figure out is when you even went to Miami."

"Last week," he said, looking away from me.

"Last week," I questioned, while trying to figure out when he had time to go all the way to Florida. "That day you claimed that you were stuck in meetings all day? You lied to me just so you could go see her?"

"Dana, I promise it wasn't like that at all. I should have said something, baby, and I regret not telling you," he said, walking closer to me. "But it's behind us now, love. I promise you that."

"How is it behind us when your face is still plastered on over TMZ?"

Picking up the remote, he unmuted the TV say that I could hear the report. Apparently, the woman who had started all of this had been admitted to a mental hospital by her sister. I listened as they played a video from the press release her sister had done.

"I would like to apologize to all of the people whose lives were affected by the lies my sister has told. This isn't the first time she's done something like this. She's very sick, mentally, and my family and I have decided to take the necessary steps to get Hazel the help she needs," the woman spoke. "We ask that you all respect our privacy during this time. Thank you."

"See," he said and turned the TV off.

"Whatever. That still doesn't excuse the fact that you lied to me, Kenyan," I said, turning to leave the room.

"I know, Dana. I can't tell you enough that I'm sorry. It won't happen again."

"Oh, I know it won't. Now let's go," I told him. "Fooling around with you, we're going to be late and the last ones to get there."

"I know you're not talking. Don't we still have to stop by your place to get your bags," he asked with a raised brow.

"Your things aren't packed either."

"Wrong. My stuff is packed and already in the car," he stated, matter-of-factly. "I packed when you were in there sleeping. You were knocked out, too. Didn't even budge."

I playfully swatted his arm and pouted. "Why did you let me sleep so long when you knew we had stuff to do."

"Nuh uh. Don't be trying to put that on me. I tried to wake you up, but you know how mean you get when somebody tries to wake you."

"Just hurry up so we can leave. I'm ready when you are."

"Okay, I'm right behind you, babe. Just let me send this stuff off to Diane."

I had never packed so fast in my life. I'm sure I had forgotten a few things, but Kenyan assured me that we could buy whatever else I needed during the trip. It wasn't like we would need much. Hell, we were headed to the beach.

****

"Oh, hell no! Baby, they're cheating," Rich said, slamming his cards down on the table.

"Ain't nobody cheating. Pick them cards up and take this spanking like a man," I teased, before slapping hands with Kenyan.

Everyone was out on the patio of the beach house we'd rented for our week here in Puerto Rican. We were in the middle of an intense game of Spades and Kenyan and I had been whooping some butt. We hadn't lost a game yet.

"Come on, baby. I need you to focus. We got this," Rich tried coaching Morgan.

"Be quiet and stop cutting my books. You're the reason we're down now," Morgan shooed him. "Dana, it's your turn."

"Gone kill 'em, baby," Kenyan laughed.

I sneakily looked at my last card before slapping it down on the table. "Booyah, baby! What you got, Rich. I know you ain't beating that."

Rich shook his head in defeat and threw his card down, followed by Kenyan and Morgan. Another win. They'd might as well give up. We had already beat Ginger and Sean, as well as Debra and Raul.

"Whoo. All that winning has made me hungry. You hungry, baby," I asked Kenyan, getting up from my seat.

"Yea, I've worked up an appetite from all those beatings we handed out," Kenyan joked along with me.

"Oh, shut up you two. No one likes a sore winner," Morgan said, throwing a chip at me.

"No one likes a sore loser either," I said, sticking my tongue out at her. "Did the chef say when dinner would be ready?"

"I think she came out and said about an hour or so. I'm going to run upstairs and take a quick shower. I have sand in places that sand shouldn't be," Morgan laughed as she stood and extended her hand out to her husband. "Come on, babe. I need help washing my back."

Richard hurried from his seat and followed behind his wife. "We'll see y'all good folks at dinner," he said, tipping his hat.

"Not so loud, you two," Ginger called behind them.

"Don't worry. We about to be doing some freaking of our own," Sean said, kissing her neck.

"Looks like we're on a trip with a bunch of freaks," I laughed, jokingly.

"Oh, don't be trying to act all innocent, Dana. Everybody heard you and Kenyan out there last night on the balcony," Debra blasted me, causing me to blush bright red. "I don't know why I pictured you as the quiet type, because you're anything but."

"Oh my god," I shrieked, covering my face in embarrassment. "See! I told you they could hear me, Kenyan!"

"You were the one talking about you wanted to do it outside because it was *romantic*," Kenyan teased me.

"You know what, I'm going inside," I laughed and left them outside.

The aroma from whatever the chef was whipping up in the kitchen permeated the air. I couldn't wait to dig in. It felt like I hadn't eaten anything all day, when not too long ago we'd had lunch. Being around Kenyan had my appetite on a thousand. It seems like all we ever did was eat. Kenyan could get away with that because he was so huge and his body required all that food. Plus, he still worked out every day. I, on the other hand, barely knew what the inside of a gym looked like. I couldn't be eating like he did. I'd already noticed that I'd put on a few pounds and they seemed to all go straight to my breast and buttocks.

"You've got it smelling good in here, Rosa," I complimented the chef.

"Thank you, Ms. Dana. You can let everyone know that dinner will be served in about thirty minutes."

"Will do. I'm just going to grab me some fruit until it's done," I said, going into the fridge to get some of the leftover fruit salad from lunch.

Kenyan was still out on the patio with Deb and Raul when I went back out there. I guess Sean was serious about what he said, because they were no longer outside. I went over and took a seat on Kenyan's lap and popped a strawberry into his awaiting mouth.

"Girl, where on earth do you store all that food," Debra asked. "I wish I could eat like that."

"Honey, I don't even need to be eating the way I do," I chuckled. "I've gained like seven pounds in the last month."

"Where," Debra asked in disbelief. "Because I sure can't tell. You look great, girl."

We sat talking about different things as Kenyan and I shared my fruit. I was about to get some more until Morgan appeared at the doorway and announced that dinner was ready. About time. Since it was so beautiful out, we decided to have dinner outside. The chef had prepared one of my favorite dishes: Bouillabaisse. I was about to dig in, but before I could have my first taste of food, a wave of nausea hit me and sent me rushing from the table. Everything I'd eaten today had come right back up. I was still hugging the toilet when someone began to knock on the door.

# Chapter 14: Kenyan

"Dana," I said, knocking on the bathroom door. "Are you okay, love? Open the door."

It sounded like she was releasing her life into that commode. I don't know where this sudden sickness was coming from, but I hoped it was temporary. She opened the door and her entire face was flushed. She looked miserable.

"What's wrong, baby?"

"I don't know. I was just fi-."

Before she could finish her sentence, she was flying back over to the toilet again. I stepped inside with her and closed the door behind me. I felt helpless right now. The only thing I could do was pull her hair back and rub her back until she was done.

"Hey," Morgan called from the other side of the door. "Is she okay?"

"Yea, she's fine. Must have eaten something that didn't agree with her. We'll be right out," I assured her.

Dana finished up and went to the sink to rinse her mouth out. She was moving in slow motion, almost as if she was afraid to make any sudden movements.

"I think I need to go lay down," she said, weakly.

"Okay. Do you think you can make it upstairs on your own?"

She looked at me with the saddest puppy-dog eyes and shook her head no. My poor baby. Swooping her up into my arms, I carried her to our room and placed her in the bed, before tucking her in.

"You don't have to stay up here with me, Kenyan. Go back downstairs and finish your dinner. I'll be okay."

"Are you sure? Do you need me to bring you anything? Maybe a ginger ale or something? Do you think you'll need to throw up again," I questioned.

"Just a cup of water, please."

"Alright. I'll be right back, love."

It was strange for her to be so sick all of a sudden. She had just been fine not even twenty minutes ago. I grabbed her phone and a bottle a water to take to her. I wanted to be sure that she could call me if she needed anything.

"She feeling okay," Morgan asked when I joined the group again.

"Yea, I think she might have caught a stomach bug or something. She's upstairs laying down right now."

"Maybe I should go check on her," she suggested.

I was already anticipating her saying that. Morgan and Dana were extremely close, so her concern was normal. She probably knew more about how to handle her at a time like this than I did. Dana had never really been sick around me, other than the occasional cold.

"Do you think that's a good idea? We don't know if what she has is contagious or not," Richard reasoned.

"I'm pretty sure it's not. I'll be back," she said, excusing herself from the table.

How was she so sure that Dana wasn't contagious? It was something about the way she said it that had me thinking that she was privy to some information that I wasn't.

"Hey, where are the keys to the van," I asked Richard.

He reached in his pocket to retrieve them. "Where you about to head?"

"Drug store. I'm going to grab Dana some ginger-ale," I said, hurrying from the table.

"I think Rosa has some in the kitchen," Debra informed me.

"Umm. Not this kind," I shot ever my shoulder.

****

After entering our suite, I almost turned around and left right back out. I'm not sure what transpired between the time it took me the run to the store, but Dana was now curled up in Morgan's arms, crying. What the hell was going on? I don't know if my hunch was correct but we were about to find out.

"Dana," I spoke, grabbing both of their attention.

She lifted her gaze to me, but quickly looked away. Morgan whispered something in her ear that caused her to shake her head viciously.

"Dana," I tried again. "Come in the bathroom with me for a minute."

"I don't have the energy to move, Kenyan," she whined.

"Then I'll carry you, but I need you to come in here," I told her.

Morgan looked to me, then back down at Dana. "I think I'll leave you two alone."

I waited until she left the room before pulling the paper bag from my coat pocket. Tossing it on the bed, I waited to see if Dana would move to see what was in it. Something told me that she already knew.

"What's that," she inquired, nervously.

"Open it, Dana."

"Why can't you just tell me what it is?"

"Dana," I called, firmly.

Huffing, she snatched up the paper bag and revealed its contents. Her eyes began to water as she held them in her hand.

"I'm not about to take these, Kenyan."

"And why not? Is there something you haven't told me?"

"There's nothing to tell and I don't need to take these," she replied, anger evident in her voice.

"So, you're telling me that you know for sure that you don't need to take one," I asked, folding my arms across my chest.

"I'm not pregnant, Kenyan!"

Her yelling caught me off guard. I wasn't expecting for the tests to upset her. I just wanted to know. I NEEDED to know.

"Love, why are you getting upset? Talk to me," I pleaded, sitting on the bed with her and taking her hands in mine.

"I'm not pregnant, Kenyan," she whispered with tears rolling down her face. "I can't be. I just can't."

"Whoa. What do you mean by that?"

Realization hit me that Dana and I had never really discussed kids. I knew for certain that I wanted to have a big family, but it never occurred to me that Dana might not be on the same page. This is something that should have been discussed because it was sort of a big issue for me.

"You don't want to have my kids, Dana?"

She began to cry hysterically. What was I supposed to do? I wanted so badly to comfort her and tell her that everything would be okay, but at the same time, I needed answers. In order for me to get those answers, Dana had to talk to me. Say something. Anything.

"Tell me something, baby," I hopefully urged.

Her eyes finally met mine and I swear the pain in her eyes made my heart ache. "What if I lose my baby again, Kenyan?"

Wait, WHAT? Again? What did she mean by again? I was more confused now than I was at first. What was she talking about? Had Dana been pregnant before?

"What do you mean again, love," I asked, cautiously.

The look on her face told me that she really didn't want to talk about this. As much as I didn't want to push her, she needed to make sense of the bomb she'd just dropped on me.

"I was pregnant, Kenyan," she sniffled.

I allowed myself time to think before I asked my next question. "When was this? Was it… Was the baby mines?"

She nodded her head as more tears fell from her eyes. I dropped my head in my hands and tried to get myself together. Dana was pregnant with my baby? A baby that she'd lost? When did all of this happen and why didn't she tell me?

"When did all this happen," I finally asked.

"Right after you left to return to school," she said, avoiding looking at me.

I stood from the bed and stared down at her incredulously. "Why the hell didn't you say something to me?"

I didn't mean to raise my voice, but that was something that she definitely should have shared with me.

"It wouldn't have mattered anyway! Not even two weeks after I found out, I lost it," she cried. "That was one of the hardest things I've ever had to deal with!"

"Dana, you still should have told me. You shouldn't have had to go through that alone. I would have been there for you. Hell, it was my baby, too."

"Kenyan, you didn't need that stress on you. We weren't together. Besides, I knew that you planned on entering the draft that year and I didn't want you to think I'd gotten pregnant on purpose to trap you."

"So, even if the baby had lived, you weren't going to tell me," I asked.

"I don't know. I didn't have time to think about that before, you know, everything happened."

Grabbing her up by her shoulders, I pulled her into my arms and held her tight. I could tell by the wetness seeping through the front of my shirt that she was still crying.

"Look, at me, Dana," I said, pulling her away from my chest. "I'm so sorry that I wasn't there for you. If I could change the past and take away all your pain, I would in a heartbeat. But I can't, baby girl. The only thing I can do is be by your side moving forward. I love you, Dana, and I'm not going anywhere."

"I love you, too, Kenyan."

I looked towards the pregnancy tests laying on the bed. There was still a big elephant in the room that needed to be addressed.

"Are you positive you don't need to take that test?"

Dana took a moment before she pulled away from me and grabbed the tests from the bed. She began to head in the direction of the bathroom, but stopped halfway there and turned to me.

"Aren't you coming with me?"

# Chapter 15: Dana

"Kenyan, for the hundredth time, I said I'm okay. Now, move," I fussed, shooing him away from me.

I swear this man had found my last nerve and he was tap-dancing on it. Every time I looked up, he was in my face asking me if I needed anything. I appreciated the care and concern, but dang, let a sister breath. I would be so happy when all of this was over with.

"Mama, please keep your son away from me before I hurt him," I told Mrs. Spencer.

"Please don't hurt him, baby," she laughed.

"See how she do me, ma," Kenyan shook his head.

"Boy, you better get on before she hurt you for real," his mom warned.

"Come out from over there, son. You're in a danger zone," his father joked.

Kenyan quickly bent down and stole a kiss before hurrying away. Lord knows I loved him, but lately it seemed like all I wanted to do was rip his head off his shoulders. My emotions were all over the place.

"Your little butt is so mean now," Morgan laughed. "I don't see how Kenyan deals with you every day."

"Shut up, Morgan. I am not mean," I said, on the brink of tears.

"Oh, lord. Why did you say that, Morgan? You know she's turned into a huge cry baby," my mother said, popping her on the leg.

"I'm not a cry baby," I whined.

They weren't about to sit up here and keep talking about me like I wasn't sitting right here.

"Kenyan," I yelled out. "Where did Kenyan go?"

I looked around the crowd of people and noticed that he was already rushing in my direction with a worried expression covering his handsome face.

"What's wrong? You okay? You need something," he fired question after question.

"I'm ready to go. They're being mean to me," I pouted.

"I know she didn't call him over here to snitch on us," my mother laughed. "Child I'm grown. What he gon' do? Whoop me?"

Kenyan laughed and shook his head. "Baby, you can't just leave. You're the guest of honor."

"Well, tell them to leave me alone."

"Y'all leave my baby alone, okay?"

"I'll be happy when your baby has these damn babies," Morgan huffed. "I don't think I can deal with a pregnant Dana too much longer."

"I swear," Charli agreed.

"You too, Charli?"

"Dee, I'm sorry, but you've been a big baby almost this entire pregnancy," Charli said, bouncing a babbling Kendra on her knee.

"I know y'all better get off my queen," Kenyan defended me. "She can act like a baby all she wants."

"Exactly why her behind is spoiled now. You better be lucky you guys are having boys or else you would really be in trouble," his mother told us.

Kenyan ignored them and squatted down beside me to talk to my stomach, a habit he'd picked up after first learning we were expecting. Some nights he would stay up to the wee hours of the morning, talking to the babies. Sometimes he would tell them stories about his childhood or how he and I met. Other times he would just talk about all the things he couldn't wait to do with them.

"Okay, mommy and daddy. It's time to open gifts," Morgan announced.

With the help of Kenyan, I got up from the seat I was in and waddled over to the royal blue and gold thrones that were placed between the blocks that spelled both of our boys' names. Kaiden and Khalil. We wanted to be sure that we stuck with the "K" tradition that his family had going on.

"You comfortable, love," Kenyan asked, after I'd taken my seat.

"Yes, I'm good baby," I assured them. "Are these chairs rentals? I want these for the nursery. They're so soft."

"Don't worry. We can make that happen," he said, kissing my lips and sitting beside me.

Morgan and Charli began passing us present after present for us to open. How many friends did we have? It seemed like there was an endless pile of gifts. After about the twentieth present, I was growing tired. Who knew opening gifts could be so draining? I had long ago stopped and let Kenyan handle the rest and just looked on with the rest of the guests. We were at the end of the pile when Kenyan picked up the last box and sat it on my lap for me to open.

I pulled the ribbon from the box and sat it on the ground. I didn't really have much room for it to sit on my lap with my stomach being all huge and everything. I removed the colorful tissue paper from the box and noticed two teddy bears sitting inside. They were both white with royal blue jerseys on them.

"Aww, these are so cute," I swooned, pulling them from the box. "Baby, look."

I took a good look and them and noticed that there was writing on the front of the one I'd pulled out first. After reading what it said, my hand flew to my mouth and I could feel the waterworks about to start.

"What is this," my voice shook.

Kenyan kneeled in front of me and removed the other bear from the box. This one had a huge question mark on the shirt and a gold velvet box in its arms.

"Oh, my word," my mother gasped in a whisper. "Is he doing what I think he's doing?"

"Yep, now hush up," my father shushed her. "I can't hear, woman."

Laughing, Kenyan turned his attention back to me and took my hand in his. I was full out boohooing by now.

"Dana," he smiled up at me. "Whew. I didn't think I would be this nervous."

"It's okay, baby. Take your time," someone called out from the crowd.

"Baby, I've been waiting to do this for a long time. Since that night at Morgan's, I knew this day would come. Even though you tried to give me a hard time at first," he joked, causing the crowd to laugh. "You don't know how happy you've made me. Every day I wake up and thank God that he brought you back to me. My life would be meaningless without you. Before, I was only existing, but because of you, I'm now living. I love you to the depths of my soul and if you agree to take my hand in marriage, I promise to love you with everything I am."

Charli discreetly passed me some Kleenex to clean my face, which I'm sure looked a hot mess right now. No way did my makeup last through all this crying I was doing. Kenyan knew I was too emotional for all this.

I watched as he released a breath and shook his nerves off before looking me square in the eyes. "So, what do you say? Dana, will you marry me?"

"Yes," I excitedly released, pulling myself from my seat as best as I could and throwing myself in his arms.

"Whoa! Be careful," Kenyan warned while steadying me. "You better not hurt my babies, woman."

What he said was going in one ear and out the other because I was too busy admiring the beautiful ring that he'd just slipped on my finger. I wasn't a big fan of jewelry, but I'd never seen such a magnificent piece in all my life. I could tell it cost a pretty penny too.

Morgan came over the mic and spoke to our guests as Kenyan and I embraced. "Everyone give it up for the newly engaged couple!"

I was smiling so hard that it felt as though my cheeks might break. Everyone was hooting and hollering, while fighting their way to see the ring. It felt good to be surrounded by so much love and support, and people who were genuinely happy for us.

"You did good, son," Mr. Spencer said, coming to pat him on the back.

"Yea, I taught him well," Kendrick joked as he joined us.

Kenyan playfully pushed his brother away from him. "Man, if you don't gon' somewhere with that. If anythi-."

"Ahhhh," I cried out and grabbed hold to the nearest person.

Kenyan was by my side in a flash. "Baby, what's wrong?"

"I think it's time, baby," I responded while trying to breathe through the pain I was experiencing.

"Right now? You sure," Kenyan asked in a panic.

No sooner than the words left his mouth, a felt a gush of warm liquid running down my legs.

"I think I'm pretty positive," I said, looking down.

"Okay, don't worry. Just stay calm. Stay calm," he said, seemingly more to himself. "We have everything ready, right? What should we do? Do I need to call your doctor? Are you having contractions?"

"Kenyan, baby, calm down," his mother soothed him. "What you need to be doing right now is getting her to the hospital? We can call her doctor on the way there. Dana, are you experiencing any pain right now?"

"Just a lot of discomfort."

"Okay," she nodded. "Let's get you out of here."

"I'll load all the gifts and everything up and meet you guys at the hospital," Kendrick volunteered.

"I'll help, too," Richard added. "Morg, why don't you ride with Dana."

She agreed and went to inform the rest of the guests that the baby shower was over because I was going into labor. Just about everyone had decided that they were going to follow behind us to the hospital. Boy, I hoped the hospital had a waiting room big enough.

\*\*\*\*

I sat propped up on the hospital bed, admiring my son as he slept in my arms. Kaiden Avery Spencer was perfect. From the curly mass of curls on his head, all the way down to his cute little toes. I loved everything about him the moment he came out. I looked over to my left and eyed my handsome fiancé as he held our other son, Khalil Ahmaad Spencer in his strong arms. The sight was almost comical. Kenyan was so massive and intimidating in size, yet looked so gentle and delicate as he cradled our son.

Life couldn't get any better than this. After a long eventful day, I was grateful to have this time alone with the three most important men in my life. I was a lucky girl.

"What you over there thinking about, love," Kenyan asked, breaking me from my thoughts.

"Just how crazy today has been and how incredibly lucky I am," I smiled.

"I think I'm the lucky one," Kenyan rose from his seat and came to join Kaiden and I on the tiny hospital bed.

"They're so perfect, babe," I swooned, glancing down at the two mini Kenyans.

"Just like their mama."

My eyes watered as what he'd just said sunk in. "I'm a mommy," I whispered in disbelief.

"Yep, and soon you'll be a wife."

"I love you, Kenyan."

"I love you, too, sweets," he said, placing a firm kiss to my lips. "Thank you for finding your way back to me."

# THE END

CPSIA information can be obtained
at www.ICGtesting.com
Printed in the USA
LVOW03s2018100417
530296LV00001B/82/P